WAR AND PEACE

BOOK TWELVE : 1812

By Leo Tolstoy

Double 9
BOOKS

War and Peace Book 12
by Leo Tolstoy

ISBN: 978-93-94973-99-2

Published by

DOUBLE 9 BOOKS

2/13-B, Ansari Road
Daryaganj, New Delhi - 110002
info@double9books.com
www.double9books.com
Tel. 011-40042856

Printed in India.

About the Author

L eo Tolstoy was a Russian creator known for his books
War and Peace which is viewed as the best book of
pragmatist fiction. Tolstoy is additionally viewed as world's
best author by quite a few people. Additionally an ethical
scholar and a social reformer, Tolstoy had extreme moralistic
points of view. In later life, he turned into an intense Christian
rebel and anarcho-conservative.

Leo Tolstoy Born in Yasnaya Polyana on September
9, 1828, He had a place with a notable honorable Russian
family. He was the fourth among five offspring of Count
Nikolai Ilyich Tolstoy and Countess Mariya Tolstaya, both of
whom kicked the bucket passing on their youngsters to be
raised by family members.

In 1844, Tolstoy was acknowledged into Kazan
University. Incapable to graduate past the subsequent year,
Tolstoy got back to Yasnava Polyana and afterward invested
energy going among Moscow and St. Petersburg. With some
functioning information on a few dialects, he turned into a
multilingual. Yet again the recently observed youth pulled in
Tolstoy towards drinking, visiting massage parlors and most
betting which left him in weighty obligation and anguish
however Tolstoy before long acknowledged he was carrying
on with a brutish life and endeavored college tests with
the expectation that he would acquire a situation with the
public authority, yet finished yet up in Caucuses serving in
the military continuing in the strides of his senior sibling.

In Year 1862, Leo Tolstoy wedded Sophia Andreevna
Behrs, generally called Sonya, who was 16 years more
youthful than him. The couple had thirteen youngsters, of

which, five passed on at an early age. Sonya went about as Tolstoy's secretary, editor and monetary chief while he made two out of his most prominent works. Their initial wedded life was loaded up with happiness.

He started composing his show-stopper, War and Peace in 1862. The six volumes of the work were distributed somewhere in the range of 1863 and 1869. With 580 characters got from history and others made by Tolstoy, this extraordinary novel takes on investigating the hypothesis of history and the irrelevance of noted figures like Alexander and Napoleon. Anna Karenina, Tolstoy's next epic was begun in 1873 and distributed totally in 1878.

Contents

BOOK TWELVE : 1812

CHAPTER I

In Petersburg at that time a complicated struggle was being carried on with greater heat than ever in the highest circles, between the parties of Rumyántsev, the French, MáryaFëdorovna, the Tsarévich, and others, drowned as usual by the buzzing of the court drones. But the calm, luxurious life of Petersburg, concerned only about phantoms and reflections of real life, went on in its old way and made it hard, except by a great effort, to realize the danger and the difficult position of the Russian people. There were the same receptions and balls, the same French theater, the same court interests and service interests and intrigues as usual. Only in the very highest circles were attempts made to keep in mind the difficulties of the actual position. Stories were whispered of how differently the two Empresses behaved in these difficult circumstances. The Empress Márya, concerned for the welfare of the charitable and educational institutions under her patronage, had given directions that they should all be removed to Kazán, and the things belonging to these institutions had already been packed up. The Empress Elisabeth, however, when asked what instructions she would be pleased to give—with her characteristic Russian patriotism had replied that she could give no directions about state institutions for that was the affair of the sovereign, but as far as she personally was concerned she would be the last to quit Petersburg.

At Anna Pávlovna's on the twenty-sixth of August, the very day of the battle of Borodinó, there was a soiree, the chief feature of which was to be the reading of a letter from His Lordship the Bishop when sending the Emperor an icon of the Venerable Sergius. It was regarded as a model of ecclesiastical, patriotic eloquence.

Prince Vasíli himself, famed for his elocution, was to read it. (He used to read at the Empress'.) The art of his reading was supposed to lie in rolling out the words, quite independently of their meaning, in a loud and singsong voice alternating between a despairing wail and a tender murmur, so that the wail fell quite at random on one word and the murmur on another. This reading, as was always the case at Anna Pávlovna's soirees, had a political significance. That evening she expected several important personages who had to be made ashamed of their visits to the French theater and aroused to a patriotic temper. A good many people had already arrived, but Anna Pávlovna, not yet seeing all those whom she wanted in her drawing room, did not let the reading begin but wound up the springs of a general conversation.

The news of the day in Petersburg was the illness of Countess Bezúkhova. She had fallen ill unexpectedly a few days previously, had missed several gatherings of which she was usually the ornament, and was said to be receiving no one, and instead of the celebrated Petersburg doctors who usually attended her had entrusted herself to some Italian doctor who was treating her in some new and unusual way.

They all knew very well that the enchanting countess' illness arose from an inconvenience resulting from marrying two husbands at the same time, and that the Italian's cure consisted in removing such inconvenience; but in Anna Pávlovna's presence no one dared to think of this or even appear to know it.

"They say the poor countess is very ill. The doctor says it is angina pectoris."

"Angina? Oh, that's a terrible illness!"

"They say that the rivals are reconciled, thanks to the angina..." and the word *angina* was repeated with great satisfaction.

"The count is pathetic, they say. He cried like a child when the doctor told him the case was dangerous."

"Oh, it would be a terrible loss, she is an enchanting woman."

"You are speaking of the poor countess?" said Anna Pávlovna, coming up just then. "I sent to ask for news, and hear that she is a little better. Oh, she is certainly the most charming woman in the world," she went on, with a smile at her own enthusiasm. "We belong to different camps, but that does not prevent my esteeming her as she deserves. She is very unfortunate!" added Anna Pávlovna.

Supposing that by these words Anna Pávlovna was somewhat lifting the veil from the secret of the countess' malady, an unwary young man ventured to express surprise that well-known doctors had not been called in and that the countess was being attended by a charlatan who might employ dangerous remedies.

"Your information may be better than mine," Anna Pávlovna suddenly and venomously retorted on the inexperienced young man, "but I know on good authority that this doctor is a very learned and able man. He is private physician to the Queen of Spain."

And having thus demolished the young man, Anna Pávlovna turned to another group where Bilíbin was talking about the Austrians: having wrinkled up his face he was evidently preparing to smooth it out again and utter one of his mots.

"I think it is delightful," he said, referring to a diplomatic note that had been sent to Vienna with some Austrian banners captured from the French by Wittgenstein, "the hero of Petropol" as he was then called in Petersburg.

"What? What's that?" asked Anna Pávlovna, securing silence for the mot, which she had heard before.

And Bilíbin repeated the actual words of the diplomatic dispatch, which he had himself composed.

"The Emperor returns these Austrian banners," said Bilíbin, "friendly banners gone astray and found on a wrong path," and his brow became smooth again.

"Charming, charming!" observed Prince Vasíli.

"The path to Warsaw, perhaps," Prince Hippolyte remarked loudly and unexpectedly. Everybody looked at him, understanding what he meant. Prince Hippolyte himself glanced around with amused surprise. He knew no more than the others what his words meant. During his diplomatic career he had more than once noticed that such utterances were received as very witty, and at every opportunity he uttered in that way the first words that entered his head. "It may turn out very well," he thought, "but if not, they'll know how to arrange matters." And really, during the awkward silence that ensued, that insufficiently patriotic person entered whom Anna Pávlovna had been waiting for and wished to convert, and she, smiling and shaking a finger at Hippolyte, invited Prince Vasíli to the table and bringing him two candles and the manuscript begged him to begin. Everyone became silent.

"Most Gracious Sovereign and Emperor!" Prince Vasíli sternly declaimed, looking round at his audience as if to inquire whether anyone had anything to say to the contrary. But no one said anything. "Moscow, our ancient capital, the New Jerusalem, receives *her* Christ"—he placed a sudden emphasis on the word *her*—"as a mother receives her zealous sons into her arms, and through the gathering mists, foreseeing the brilliant glory of thy rule, sings in exultation, 'Hosanna, blessed is he that cometh!'"

Prince Vasíli pronounced these last words in a tearful voice.

Bilíbin attentively examined his nails, and many of those present appeared intimidated, as if asking in what they were to blame. Anna Pávlovna whispered the next words in advance, like an old woman muttering the prayer at Communion: "Let the bold and insolent Goliath..." she whispered.

Prince Vasíli continued.

"Let the bold and insolent Goliath from the borders of France encompass the realms of Russia with death-bearing terrors; humble Faith, the sling of the Russian David, shall suddenly smite his head in his bloodthirsty pride. This icon of the Venerable Sergius, the servant of God and zealous champion of old of our country's weal, is offered to Your Imperial Majesty. I grieve that my waning strength prevents rejoicing in the sight of your most gracious presence. I raise fervent prayers to Heaven that the Almighty may exalt the race of the just, and mercifully fulfill the desires of Your Majesty."

"What force! What a style!" was uttered in approval both of reader and of author.

Animated by that address Anna Pávlovna's guests talked for a long time of the state of the fatherland and offered various conjectures as to the result of the battle to be fought in a few days.

"You will see," said Anna Pávlovna, "that tomorrow, on the Emperor's birthday, we shall receive news. I have a favorable presentiment!"

CHAPTER II

Anna Pávlovna's presentiment was in fact fulfilled. Next day during the service at the palace church in honor of the Emperor's birthday, Prince Volkónski was called out of the church and received a dispatch from Prince Kutúzov. It was Kutúzov's report, written from Tatárinova on the day of the battle. Kutúzov wrote that the Russians had not retreated a step, that the French losses were much heavier than ours, and that he was writing in haste from the field of battle before collecting full information. It followed that there must have been a victory. And at once, without leaving the church, thanks were rendered to the Creator for His help and for the victory.

Anna Pávlovna's presentiment was justified, and all that morning a joyously festive mood reigned in the city. Everyone believed the victory to have been complete, and some even spoke of Napoleon's having been captured, of his deposition, and of the choice of a new ruler for France.

It is very difficult for events to be reflected in their real strength and completeness amid the conditions of court life and far from the scene of action. General events involuntarily group themselves around some particular incident. So now the courtiers' pleasure was based as much on the fact that the news had arrived on the Emperor's birthday as on the fact of the victory itself. It was like a successfully arranged surprise. Mention was made in Kutúzov's report of the Russian losses, among which figured the names of Túchkov, Bagratión, and Kutáysov. In the Petersburg world this sad side of the affair again involuntarily centered round a single incident:

Kutáysov's death. Everybody knew him, the Emperor liked him, and he was young and interesting. That day everyone met with the words:

"What a wonderful coincidence! Just during the service. But what a loss Kutáysov is! How sorry I am!"

"What did I tell about Kutúzov?" Prince Vasíli now said with a prophet's pride. "I always said he was the only man capable of defeating Napoleon."

But next day no news arrived from the army and the public mood grew anxious. The courtiers suffered because of the suffering the suspense occasioned the Emperor.

"Fancy the Emperor's position!" said they, and instead of extolling Kutúzov as they had done the day before, they condemned him as the cause of the Emperor's anxiety. That day Prince Vasíli no longer boasted of his protégé Kutúzov, but remained silent when the commander in chief was mentioned. Moreover, toward evening, as if everything conspired to make Petersburg society anxious and uneasy, a terrible piece of news was added. Countess Hélène Bezúkhova had suddenly died of that terrible malady it had been so agreeable to mention. Officially, at large gatherings, everyone said that Countess Bezúkhova had died of a terrible attack of angina pectoris, but in intimate circles details were mentioned of how the private physician of the Queen of Spain had prescribed small doses of a certain drug to produce a certain effect; but Hélène, tortured by the fact that the old count suspected her and that her husband to whom she had written (that wretched, profligate Pierre) had not replied, had suddenly taken a very large dose of the drug, and had died in agony before assistance could be rendered her. It was said that Prince Vasíli and the old count had turned upon the Italian, but the latter had produced such letters from the unfortunate deceased that they had immediately let the matter drop.

Talk in general centered round three melancholy facts: the Emperor's lack of news, the loss of Kutáysov, and the death of Hélène.

On the third day after Kutúzov's report a country gentleman arrived from Moscow, and news of the surrender of Moscow to the French spread through the whole town. This was terrible! What a position for the Emperor to be in! Kutúzov was a traitor, and Prince Vasíli during the visits of condolence paid to him on the occasion of his daughter's death said of Kutúzov, whom he had formerly praised (it was excusable for him in his grief to forget what he had said), that it was impossible to expect anything else from a blind and depraved old man.

"I only wonder that the fate of Russia could have been entrusted to such a man."

As long as this news remained unofficial it was possible to doubt it, but the next day the following communication was received from Count Rostopchín:

Prince Kutúzov's adjutant has brought me a letter in which he demands police officers to guide the army to the Ryazán road. He writes that he is regretfully abandoning Moscow. Sire! Kutúzov's action decides the fate of the capital and of your empire! Russia will shudder to learn of the abandonment of the city in which her greatness is centered and in which lie the ashes of your ancestors! I shall follow the army. I have had everything removed, and it only remains for me to weep over the fate of my fatherland.

On receiving this dispatch the Emperor sent Prince Volkónski to Kutúzov with the following rescript:

Prince Michael Ilariónovich! Since the twenty-ninth of August I have received no communication from you, yet on the first of September I received from the commander in chief of Moscow, via Yaroslávl, the sad news that you, with the army, have decided to abandon Moscow. You can yourself imagine the effect this news has had on me, and your silence increases my astonishment. I am sending this by Adjutant-General Prince Volkónski, to hear from you the situation of the army and the reasons that have induced you to take this melancholy decision.

CHAPTER III

Nine days after the abandonment of Moscow, a messenger from Kutúzov reached Petersburg with the official announcement of that event. This messenger was Michaud, a Frenchman who did not know Russian, but who was *quoique étranger, russe de cœur et d'âme,* * as he said of himself.

* Though a foreigner, Russian in heart and soul.

The Emperor at once received this messenger in his study at the palace on Stone Island. Michaud, who had never seen Moscow before the campaign and who did not know Russian, yet felt deeply moved (as he wrote) when he appeared before *notretrèsgracieux souverain* * with the news of the burning of Moscow, *dont les flammeséclairaientsa route.* *(2)

* Our most gracious sovereign.

* (2) Whose flames illumined his route.

Though the source of M. Michaud's chagrin must have been different from that which caused Russians to grieve, he had such a sad face when shown into the Emperor's study that the latter at once asked:

"Have you brought me sad news, Colonel?"

"Very sad, sire," replied Michaud, lowering his eyes with a sigh. "The abandonment of Moscow."

"Have they surrendered my ancient capital without a battle?" asked the Emperor quickly, his face suddenly flushing.

Michaud respectfully delivered the message Kutúzov had entrusted to him, which was that it had been impossible to fight before Moscow, and that as the only remaining choice was between losing the army as well as Moscow, or losing Moscow alone, the field marshal had to choose the latter.

The Emperor listened in silence, not looking at Michaud.

"Has the enemy entered the city?" he asked.

"Yes, sire, and Moscow is now in ashes. I left it all in flames," replied Michaud in a decided tone, but glancing at the Emperor he was frightened by what he had done.

The Emperor began to breathe heavily and rapidly, his lower lip trembled, and tears instantly appeared in his fine blue eyes.

But this lasted only a moment. He suddenly frowned, as if blaming himself for his weakness, and raising his head addressed Michaud in a firm voice:

"I see, Colonel, from all that is happening, that Providence requires great sacrifices of us... I am ready to submit myself in all things to His will; but tell me, Michaud, how did you leave the army when it saw my ancient capital abandoned without a battle? Did you not notice discouragement?..."

Seeing that his most gracious ruler was calm once more, Michaud also grew calm, but was not immediately ready to reply to the Emperor's direct and relevant question which required a direct answer.

"Sire, will you allow me to speak frankly as befits a loyal soldier?" he asked to gain time.

"Colonel, I always require it," replied the Emperor. "Conceal nothing from me, I wish to know absolutely how things are."

"Sire!" said Michaud with a subtle, scarcely perceptible smile on his lips, having now prepared a well-phrased reply, "sire, I left the whole army, from its chiefs to the lowest soldier, without exception in desperate and agonized terror..."

"How is that?" the Emperor interrupted him, frowning sternly. "Would misfortune make my Russians lose heart?... Never!"

Michaud had only waited for this to bring out the phrase he had prepared.

"Sire," he said, with respectful playfulness, "they are only afraid lest Your Majesty, in the goodness of your heart, should allow yourself to be persuaded to make peace. They are burning for the combat," declared this representative of the Russian nation, "and to prove to Your Majesty by the sacrifice of their lives how devoted they are...."

"Ah!" said the Emperor reassured, and with a kindly gleam in his eyes, he patted Michaud on the shoulder. "You set me at ease, Colonel."

He bent his head and was silent for some time.

"Well, then, go back to the army," he said, drawing himself up to his full height and addressing Michaud with a gracious and majestic gesture, "and tell our brave men and all my good subjects wherever you go that when I have not a soldier left I shall put myself at the head of my beloved nobility and my good peasants and so use the last resources of my empire. It still offers me more than my enemies suppose," said the Emperor growing more and more animated; "but should it ever be ordained by Divine Providence," he continued, raising to heaven his fine eyes shining with emotion, "that my dynasty should cease to reign on the throne of my ancestors, then after exhausting all the means at my command, I shall let my beard grow to here" (he pointed halfway down his chest) "and go and eat potatoes with the meanest of my peasants, rather than sign the disgrace of my country and of my beloved people whose sacrifices I know how to appreciate."

Having uttered these words in an agitated voice the Emperor suddenly turned away as if to hide from Michaud the tears that rose to his eyes, and went to the further end of his study. Having stood there a few moments, he strode back to Michaud and pressed his arm below the elbow with a vigorous movement. The Emperor's mild and handsome face was flushed and his eyes gleamed with resolution and anger.

"Colonel Michaud, do not forget what I say to you here, perhaps we may recall it with pleasure someday... Napoleon or I," said the Emperor, touching his breast. "We can no longer both reign together. I have learned to know him, and he will not deceive me any more...."

And the Emperor paused, with a frown.

When he heard these words and saw the expression of firm resolution in the Emperor's eyes, Michaud—*quoique étranger, russe de cœur et d'âme,*—at that solemn moment felt himself enraptured by all that he had heard (as he used afterwards to say), and gave expression to his own feelings and those of the Russian people whose representative he considered himself to be, in the following words:

"Sire!" said he, "Your Majesty is at this moment signing the glory of the nation and the salvation of Europe!"

With an inclination of the head the Emperor dismissed him.

CHAPTER IV

I t is natural for us who were not living in those days to imagine that when half Russia had been conquered and the inhabitants were fleeing to distant provinces, and one levy after another was being raised for the defense of the fatherland, all Russians from the greatest to the least were solely engaged in sacrificing themselves, saving their fatherland, or weeping over its downfall. The tales and descriptions of that time without exception speak only of the self-sacrifice, patriotic devotion, despair, grief, and the heroism of the Russians. But it was not really so. It appears so to us because we see only the general historic interest of that time and do not see all the personal human interests that people had. Yet in reality those personal interests of the moment so much transcend the general interests that they always prevent the public interest from being felt or even noticed. Most of the people at that time paid no attention to the general progress of events but were guided only by their private interests, and they were the very people whose activities at that period were most useful.

Those who tried to understand the general course of events and to take part in it by self-sacrifice and heroism were the most useless members of society, they saw everything upside down, and all they did for the common good turned out to be useless and foolish—like Pierre's and Mamónov's regiments which looted Russian villages, and the lint the young ladies prepared and that never reached the wounded, and so on. Even those, fond of intellectual talk and of expressing their feelings, who discussed Russia's position at the time involuntarily introduced into their conversation either a shade of pretense and falsehood or useless condemnation and anger directed against people accused of actions no one could possibly be guilty of.

In historic events the rule forbidding us to eat of the fruit of the Tree of Knowledge is specially applicable. Only unconscious action bears fruit, and he who plays a part in an historic event never understands its significance. If he tries to realize it his efforts are fruitless.

The more closely a man was engaged in the events then taking place in Russia the less did he realize their significance. In Petersburg and in the provinces at a distance from Moscow, ladies, and gentlemen in militia uniforms, wept for Russia and its ancient capital and talked of self-sacrifice and so on; but in the army which retired beyond Moscow there was little talk or thought of Moscow, and when they caught sight of its burned ruins no one swore to be avenged on the French, but they thought about their next pay, their next quarters, of Matrëshka the vivandière, and like matters.

As the war had caught him in the service, Nicholas Rostóv took a close and prolonged part in the defense of his country, but did so casually, without any aim at self-sacrifice, and he therefore looked at what was going on in Russia without despair and without dismally racking his brains over it. Had he been asked what he thought of the state of Russia, he would have said that it was not his business to think about it, that Kutúzov and others were there for that purpose, but that he had heard that the regiments were to be made up to their full strength, that fighting would probably go on for a long time yet, and that things being so it was quite likely he might be in command of a regiment in a couple of years' time.

As he looked at the matter in this way, he learned that he was being sent to Vorónezh to buy remounts for his division, not only without regret at being prevented from taking part in the coming battle, but with the greatest pleasure—which he did not conceal and which his comrades fully understood.

A few days before the battle of Borodinó, Nicholas received the necessary money and warrants, and having sent some hussars on in advance, he set out with post horses for Vorónezh.

Only a man who has experienced it—that is, has passed some months continuously in an atmosphere of campaigning and war—can understand the delight Nicholas felt when he escaped from the region covered by the army's foraging operations, provision trains, and hospitals. When—free from soldiers, wagons, and the filthy traces of a camp—he saw villages with peasants and peasant women, gentlemen's country houses, fields where cattle were grazing, posthouses with stationmasters asleep in them, he rejoiced as though seeing all this for the first time. What for a long while specially surprised and delighted him were the women, young and healthy, without a dozen officers making up to each of them; women, too, who were pleased and flattered that a passing officer should joke with them.

In the highest spirits Nicholas arrived at night at a hotel in Vorónezh, ordered things he had long been deprived of in camp, and next day, very clean-shaven and in a full-dress uniform he had not worn for a long time, went to present himself to the authorities.

The commander of the militia was a civilian general, an old man who was evidently pleased with his military designation and rank. He received Nicholas brusquely (imagining this to be characteristically military) and questioned him with an important air, as if considering the general progress of affairs and approving and disapproving with full right to do so. Nicholas was in such good spirits that this merely amused him.

From the commander of the militia he drove to the governor. The governor was a brisk little man, very simple and affable. He indicated the stud farms at which Nicholas might procure horses, recommended to him a horse dealer in the town and a landowner fourteen miles out of town who had the best horses, and promised to assist him in every way.

"You are Count IlyáRostóv's son? My wife was a great friend of your mother's. We are at home on Thursdays—today is Thursday, so please come and see us quite informally," said the governor, taking leave of him.

Immediately on leaving the governor's, Nicholas hired post horses and, taking his squadron quartermaster with him, drove at a gallop to the landowner, fourteen miles away, who had the stud. Everything seemed to him pleasant and easy during that first part of his stay in Vorónezh and, as usually happens when a man is in a pleasant state of mind, everything went well and easily.

The landowner to whom Nicholas went was a bachelor, an old cavalryman, a horse fancier, a sportsman, the possessor of some century-old brandy and some old Hungarian wine, who had a snuggery where he smoked, and who owned some splendid horses.

In very few words Nicholas bought seventeen picked stallions for six thousand rubles—to serve, as he said, as samples of his remounts. After dining and taking rather too much of the Hungarian wine, Nicholas—having exchanged kisses with the landowner, with whom he was already on the friendliest terms—galloped back over abominable roads, in the brightest frame of mind, continually urging on the driver so as to be in time for the governor's party.

When he had changed, poured water over his head, and scented himself, Nicholas arrived at the governor's rather late, but with the phrase "better late than never" on his lips.

It was not a ball, nor had dancing been announced, but everyone knew that Catherine Petróvna would play valses and the *écossaise* on the clavichord and that there would be dancing, and so everyone had come as to a ball.

Provincial life in 1812 went on very much as usual, but with this difference, that it was livelier in the towns in consequence of the arrival of many wealthy families from Moscow, and as in everything that went on in Russia at that time a special recklessness was noticeable, an "in for a penny, in for a pound—who cares?" spirit, and the inevitable small talk, instead of turning on the weather and mutual acquaintances, now turned on Moscow, the army, and Napoleon.

The society gathered together at the governor's was the best in Vorónezh.

There were a great many ladies and some of Nicholas' Moscow acquaintances, but there were no men who could at all vie with the cavalier of St. George, the hussar remount officer, the good-natured and well-bred Count Rostóv. Among the men was an Italian prisoner, an officer of the French army; and Nicholas felt that the presence of that prisoner enhanced his own importance as a Russian hero. The Italian was, as it were, a war trophy. Nicholas felt this, it seemed to him that everyone regarded the Italian in the same light, and he treated him cordially though with dignity and restraint.

As soon as Nicholas entered in his hussar uniform, diffusing around him a fragrance of perfume and wine, and had uttered the words "better late than never" and heard them repeated several times by others, people clustered around him; all eyes turned on him, and he felt at once that he had entered into his proper position in the province—that of a universal favorite: a very pleasant position, and intoxicatingly so after his long privations. At posting stations, at inns, and in the landowner's snuggery, maidservants had been flattered by his notice, and here too at the governor's party there were (as it seemed to Nicholas) an inexhaustible number of pretty young women, married and unmarried, impatiently awaiting his notice. The women and girls flirted with him and, from the first day, the people concerned themselves to get this fine young daredevil of an hussar married and settled down. Among these was the governor's wife herself, who welcomed Rostóv as a near relative and called him "Nicholas."

Catherine Petróvna did actually play valses and the *écossaise*, and dancing began in which Nicholas still further captivated the provincial society by his agility. His particularly free manner of dancing even surprised them all. Nicholas was himself rather surprised at the way he danced that evening. He had never danced like that in Moscow and would even have considered such a very free and easy manner improper and in bad form, but here he felt it incumbent on him to astonish them all by something unusual, something they would have to accept as the regular thing in the capital though new to them in the provinces.

All the evening Nicholas paid attention to a blue-eyed, plump and pleasing little blonde, the wife of one of the provincial officials. With the naïve conviction of young men in a merry mood that other men's wives were created for them, Rostóv did not leave the lady's side and treated her husband in a friendly and conspiratorial style, as if, without speaking of it, they knew how capitally Nicholas and the lady would get on together. The husband, however, did not seem to share that conviction and tried to behave morosely with Rostóv. But the latter's good-natured naïveté was so boundless that sometimes even he involuntarily yielded to Nicholas' good humor. Toward the end of the evening, however, as the wife's face grew more flushed and animated, the husband's became more and more melancholy and solemn, as though there were but a given amount of animation between them and as the wife's share increased the husband's diminished.

CHAPTER V

Nicholas sat leaning slightly forward in an armchair, bending closely over the blonde lady and paying her mythological compliments with a smile that never left his face. Jauntily shifting the position of his legs in their tight riding breeches, diffusing an odor of perfume, and admiring his partner, himself, and the fine outlines of his legs in their well-fitting Hessian boots, Nicholas told the blonde lady that he wished to run away with a certain lady here in Vorónezh.

"Which lady?"

"A charming lady, a divine one. Her eyes" (Nicholas looked at his partner) "are blue, her mouth coral and ivory; her figure" (he glanced at her shoulders) "like Diana's...."

The husband came up and sullenly asked his wife what she was talking about.

"Ah, NikítaIványch!" cried Nicholas, rising politely, and as if wishing NikítaIványch to share his joke, he began to tell him of his intention to elope with a blonde lady.

The husband smiled gloomily, the wife gaily. The governor's good-natured wife came up with a look of disapproval.

"Anna Ignátyevna wants to see you, Nicholas," said she, pronouncing the name so that Nicholas at once understood that Anna Ignátyevna was a very important person. "Come, Nicholas! You know you let me call you so?"

"Oh, yes, Aunt. Who is she?"

"Anna IgnátyevnaMalvíntseva. She has heard from her niece how you rescued her.... Can you guess?"

"I rescued such a lot of them!" said Nicholas.

"Her niece, Princess Bolkónskaya. She is here in Vorónezh with her aunt. Oho! How you blush. Why, are...?"

"Not a bit! Please don't, Aunt!"

"Very well, very well!... Oh, what a fellow you are!"

The governor's wife led him up to a tall and very stout old lady with a blue headdress, who had just finished her game of cards with the most important personages of the town. This was Malvíntseva, Princess Mary's aunt on her mother's side, a rich, childless widow who always lived in Vorónezh. When Rostóv approached her she was standing settling up for the game. She looked at him and, screwing up her eyes sternly, continued to upbraid the general who had won from her.

"Very pleased, *moncher*," she then said, holding out her hand to Nicholas. "Pray come and see me."

After a few words about Princess Mary and her late father, whom Malvíntseva had evidently not liked, and having asked what Nicholas knew of Prince Andrew, who also was evidently no favorite of hers, the important old lady dismissed Nicholas after repeating her invitation to come to see her.

Nicholas promised to come and blushed again as he bowed. At the mention of Princess Mary he experienced a feeling of shyness and even of fear, which he himself did not understand.

When he had parted from Malvíntseva Nicholas wished to return to the dancing, but the governor's little wife placed her plump hand on his sleeve and, saying that she wanted to have a talk with him, led him to her sitting room, from which those who were there immediately withdrew so as not to be in her way.

"Do you know, dear boy," began the governor's wife with a serious expression on her kind little face, "that really would be the match for you: would you like me to arrange it?"

"Whom do you mean, Aunt?" asked Nicholas.

"I will make a match for you with the princess. Catherine Petróvna speaks of Lily, but I say, no—the princess! Do you want me to do it? I am sure your mother will be grateful to me. What a charming girl she is, really! And she is not at all so plain, either."

"Not at all," replied Nicholas as if offended at the idea. "As befits a soldier, Aunt, I don't force myself on anyone or refuse anything," he said before he had time to consider what he was saying.

"Well then, remember, this is not a joke!"

"Of course not!"

"Yes, yes," the governor's wife said as if talking to herself. "But, my dear boy, among other things you are too attentive to the other, the blonde. One is sorry for the husband, really...."

"Oh no, we are good friends with him," said Nicholas in the simplicity of his heart; it did not enter his head that a pastime so pleasant to himself might not be pleasant to someone else.

"But what nonsense I have been saying to the governor's wife!" thought Nicholas suddenly at supper. "She will really begin to arrange a match... and Sónya...?" And on taking leave of the governor's wife, when she again smilingly said to him, "Well then, remember!" he drew her aside.

"But see here, to tell the truth, Aunt..."

"What is it, my dear? Come, let's sit down here," said she.

Nicholas suddenly felt a desire and need to tell his most intimate thoughts (which he would not have told to his mother, his sister, or his friend) to this woman who was almost a stranger. When he afterwards recalled that impulse to unsolicited and inexplicable frankness which had very important results for him, it seemed to him—as it seems to everyone in such cases—that it was merely some silly whim that seized him: yet that burst of frankness, together with other trifling events, had immense consequences for him and for all his family.

"You see, Aunt, Mamma has long wanted me to marry an heiress, but the very idea of marrying for money is repugnant to me."

"Oh yes, I understand," said the governor's wife.

"But Princess Bolkónskaya—that's another matter. I will tell you the truth. In the first place I like her very much, I feel drawn to her; and then, after I met her under such circumstances—so strangely, the idea often occurred to me: 'This is fate.' Especially if you remember that Mamma had long been thinking of it; but I had never happened to meet her before, somehow it had always happened that we did not meet. And as long as my sister Natásha was engaged to her brother it was of course out of the question for me to think of marrying her. And it must needs happen that I should meet her just when Natásha's engagement had been broken off... and then everything... So you see... I never told this to anyone and never will, only to you."

The governor's wife pressed his elbow gratefully.

"You know Sónya, my cousin? I love her, and promised to marry her, and will do so.... So you see there can be no question about—" said Nicholas incoherently and blushing.

"My dear boy, what a way to look at it! You know Sónya has nothing and you yourself say your Papa's affairs are in a very bad way. And what about your mother? It would kill her, that's one thing. And what sort of life would it be for Sónya—if she's a girl with a heart? Your mother in despair, and you all ruined.... No, my dear, you and Sónya ought to understand that."

Nicholas remained silent. It comforted him to hear these arguments.

"All the same, Aunt, it is impossible," he rejoined with a sigh, after a short pause. "Besides, would the princess have me? And besides, she is now in mourning. How can one think of it!"

"But you don't suppose I'm going to get you married at once? There is always a right way of doing things," replied the governor's wife.

"What a matchmaker you are, Aunt..." said Nicholas, kissing her plump little hand.

CHAPTER VI

On reaching Moscow after her meeting with Rostóv, Princess Mary had found her nephew there with his tutor, and a letter from Prince Andrew giving her instructions how to get to her Aunt Malvíntseva at Vorónezh. That feeling akin to temptation which had tormented her during her father's illness, since his death, and especially since her meeting with Rostóv was smothered by arrangements for the journey, anxiety about her brother, settling in a new house, meeting new people, and attending to her nephew's education. She was sad. Now, after a month passed in quiet surroundings, she felt more and more deeply the loss of her father which was associated in her mind with the ruin of Russia. She was agitated and incessantly tortured by the thought of the dangers to which her brother, the only intimate person now remaining to her, was exposed. She was worried too about her nephew's education for which she had always felt herself incompetent, but in the depths of her soul she felt at peace—a peace arising from consciousness of having stifled those personal dreams and hopes that had been on the point of awakening within her and were related to her meeting with Rostóv.

The day after her party the governor's wife came to see Malvíntseva and, after discussing her plan with the aunt, remarked that though under present circumstances a formal betrothal was, of course, not to be thought of, all the same the young people might be brought together and could get to know one another. Malvíntseva expressed approval, and the governor's wife began to speak of Rostóv in Mary's presence, praising him and telling how he had blushed when Princess Mary's name was mentioned. But Princess

Mary experienced a painful rather than a joyful feeling—her mental tranquillity was destroyed, and desires, doubts, self-reproach, and hopes reawoke.

During the two days that elapsed before Rostóv called, Princess Mary continually thought of how she ought to behave to him. First she decided not to come to the drawing room when he called to see her aunt—that it would not be proper for her, in her deep mourning, to receive visitors; then she thought this would be rude after what he had done for her; then it occurred to her that her aunt and the governor's wife had intentions concerning herself and Rostóv—their looks and words at times seemed to confirm this supposition—then she told herself that only she, with her sinful nature, could think this of them: they could not forget that situated as she was, while still wearing deep mourning, such matchmaking would be an insult to her and to her father's memory. Assuming that she did go down to see him, Princess Mary imagined the words he would say to her and what she would say to him, and these words sometimes seemed undeservedly cold and then to mean too much. More than anything she feared lest the confusion she felt might overwhelm her and betray her as soon as she saw him.

But when on Sunday after church the footman announced in the drawing room that Count Rostóv had called, the princess showed no confusion, only a slight blush suffused her cheeks and her eyes lit up with a new and radiant light.

"You have met him, Aunt?" said she in a calm voice, unable herself to understand that she could be outwardly so calm and natural.

When Rostóv entered the room, the princess dropped her eyes for an instant, as if to give the visitor time to greet her aunt, and then just as Nicholas turned to her she raised her head and met his look with shining eyes. With a movement full of dignity and grace she half rose with a smile of pleasure, held out her slender, delicate hand to him, and began to speak in a voice in which for the first time new deep womanly notes vibrated. Mademoiselle Bourienne, who was in the drawing room, looked at Princess Mary in bewildered surprise. Herself a consummate coquette, she could not have maneuvered better on meeting a man she wished to attract.

"Either black is particularly becoming to her or she really has greatly improved without my having noticed it. And above all, what tact and grace!" thought Mademoiselle Bourienne.

Had Princess Mary been capable of reflection at that moment, she would have been more surprised than Mademoiselle Bourienne at the change that had taken place in herself. From the moment she recognized that dear, loved face, a new life force took possession of her and compelled her to speak and act apart from her own will. From the time Rostóv entered, her face became suddenly transformed. It was as if a light had been kindled in a carved and painted lantern and the intricate, skillful, artistic work on its sides, that previously seemed dark, coarse, and meaningless, was suddenly shown up in unexpected and striking beauty. For the first time all that pure, spiritual, inward travail through which she had lived appeared on the surface. All her inward labor, her dissatisfaction with herself, her sufferings, her strivings after goodness, her meekness, love, and self-sacrifice—all this now shone in those radiant eyes, in her delicate smile, and in every trait of her gentle face.

Rostóv saw all this as clearly as if he had known her whole life. He felt that the being before him was quite different from, and better than, anyone he had met before, and above all better than himself.

Their conversation was very simple and unimportant. They spoke of the war, and like everyone else unconsciously exaggerated their sorrow about it; they spoke of their last meeting—Nicholas trying to change the subject—they talked of the governor's kind wife, of Nicholas' relations, and of Princess Mary's.

She did not talk about her brother, diverting the conversation as soon as her aunt mentioned Andrew. Evidently she could speak of Russia's misfortunes with a certain artificiality, but her brother was too near her heart and she neither could nor would speak lightly of him. Nicholas noticed this, as he noticed every shade of Princess Mary's character with an observation unusual to him, and everything confirmed his conviction that she was a quite unusual and extraordinary being. Nicholas blushed and was confused when people spoke to him about the princess (as she did when he was mentioned) and even when he thought of her, but in her presence he felt quite at ease, and said not at all what he had prepared, but what, quite appropriately, occurred to him at the moment.

When a pause occurred during his short visit, Nicholas, as is usual when there are children, turned to Prince Andrew's little son, caressing him and asking whether he would like to be an hussar. He took the boy on his knee, played with him, and looked round at

Princess Mary. With a softened, happy, timid look she watched the boy she loved in the arms of the man she loved. Nicholas also noticed that look and, as if understanding it, flushed with pleasure and began to kiss the boy with good natured playfulness.

As she was in mourning Princess Mary did not go out into society, and Nicholas did not think it the proper thing to visit her again; but all the same the governor's wife went on with her matchmaking, passing on to Nicholas the flattering things Princess Mary said of him and vice versa, and insisting on his declaring himself to Princess Mary. For this purpose she arranged a meeting between the young people at the bishop's house before Mass.

Though Rostóv told the governor's wife that he would not make any declaration to Princess Mary, he promised to go.

As at Tilsit Rostóv had not allowed himself to doubt that what everybody considered right was right, so now, after a short but sincere struggle between his effort to arrange his life by his own sense of justice, and in obedient submission to circumstances, he chose the latter and yielded to the power he felt irresistibly carrying him he knew not where. He knew that after his promise to Sónya it would be what he deemed base to declare his feelings to Princess Mary. And he knew that he would never act basely. But he also knew (or rather felt at the bottom of his heart) that by resigning himself now to the force of circumstances and to those who were guiding him, he was not only doing nothing wrong, but was doing something very important—more important than anything he had ever done in his life.

After meeting Princess Mary, though the course of his life went on externally as before, all his former amusements lost their charm for him and he often thought about her. But he never thought about her as he had thought of all the young ladies without exception whom he had met in society, nor as he had for a long time, and at one time rapturously, thought about Sónya. He had pictured each of those young ladies as almost all honest-hearted young men do, that is, as a possible wife, adapting her in his imagination to all the conditions of married life: a white dressing gown, his wife at the tea table, his wife's carriage, little ones, Mamma and Papa, their relations to her, and so on—and these pictures of the future had given him pleasure. But with Princess Mary, to whom they were trying to get him engaged, he could never picture anything of future married life. If he tried, his pictures seemed incongruous and false. It made him afraid.

CHAPTER VII

The dreadful news of the battle of Borodinó, of our losses in killed and wounded, and the still more terrible news of the loss of Moscow reached Vorónezh in the middle of September. Princess Mary, having learned of her brother's wound only from the *Gazette* and having no definite news of him, prepared (so Nicholas heard, he had not seen her again himself) to set off in search of Prince Andrew.

When he received the news of the battle of Borodinó and the abandonment of Moscow, Rostóv was not seized with despair, anger, the desire for vengeance, or any feeling of that kind, but everything in Vorónezh suddenly seemed to him dull and tiresome, and he experienced an indefinite feeling of shame and awkwardness. The conversations he heard seemed to him insincere; he did not know how to judge all these affairs and felt that only in the regiment would everything again become clear to him. He made haste to finish buying the horses, and often became unreasonably angry with his servant and squadron quartermaster.

A few days before his departure a special thanksgiving, at which Nicholas was present, was held in the cathedral for the Russian victory. He stood a little behind the governor and held himself with military decorum through the service, meditating on a great variety of subjects. When the service was over the governor's wife beckoned him to her.

"Have you seen the princess?" she asked, indicating with a movement of her head a lady standing on the opposite side, beyond the choir.

Nicholas immediately recognized Princess Mary not so much by the profile he saw under her bonnet as by the feeling of solicitude, timidity, and pity that immediately overcame him. Princess Mary, evidently engrossed by her thoughts, was crossing herself for the last time before leaving the church.

Nicholas looked at her face with surprise. It was the same face he had seen before, there was the same general expression of refined, inner, spiritual labor, but now it was quite differently lit up. There was a pathetic expression of sorrow, prayer, and hope in it. As had occurred before when she was present, Nicholas went up to her without waiting to be prompted by the governor's wife and not asking himself whether or not it was right and proper to address her here in church, and told her he had heard of her trouble and sympathized with his whole soul. As soon as she heard his voice a vivid glow kindled in her face, lighting up both her sorrow and her joy.

"There is one thing I wanted to tell you, Princess," said Rostóv. "It is that if your brother, Prince Andrew Nikoláevich, were not living, it would have been at once announced in the *Gazette*, as he is a colonel."

The princess looked at him, not grasping what he was saying, but cheered by the expression of regretful sympathy on his face.

"And I have known so many cases of a splinter wound" (the *Gazette* said it was a shell) "either proving fatal at once or being very slight," continued Nicholas. "We must hope for the best, and I am sure…"

Princess Mary interrupted him.

"Oh, that would be so dread…" she began and, prevented by agitation from finishing, she bent her head with a movement as graceful as everything she did in his presence and, looking up at him gratefully, went out, following her aunt.

That evening Nicholas did not go out, but stayed at home to settle some accounts with the horse dealers. When he had finished that business it was already too late to go anywhere but still too early to go to bed, and for a long time he paced up and down the room, reflecting on his life, a thing he rarely did.

Princess Mary had made an agreeable impression on him when he had met her in Smolénsk province. His having encountered her in such exceptional circumstances, and his mother having at one time mentioned her to him as a good match, had drawn his particular attention to her. When he met her again in Vorónezh the impression she made on him was not merely pleasing but powerful. Nicholas had been struck by the peculiar moral beauty he observed in her at this time. He was, however, preparing to go away and it had not entered his head to regret that he was thus depriving himself of chances of meeting her. But that day's encounter in church had, he felt, sunk deeper than was desirable for his peace of mind. That pale, sad, refined face, that radiant look, those gentle graceful gestures, and especially the deep and tender sorrow expressed in all her features agitated him and evoked his sympathy. In men Rostóv could not bear to see the expression of a higher spiritual life (that was why he did not like Prince Andrew) and he referred to it contemptuously as philosophy and dreaminess, but in Princess Mary that very sorrow which revealed the depth of a whole spiritual world foreign to him was an irresistible attraction.

"She must be a wonderful woman. A real angel!" he said to himself. "Why am I not free? Why was I in such a hurry with Sónya?" And he involuntarily compared the two: the lack of spirituality in the one and the abundance of it in the other—a spirituality he himself lacked and therefore valued most highly. He tried to picture what would happen were he free. How he would propose to her and how she would become his wife. But no, he could not imagine that. He felt awed, and no clear picture presented itself to his mind. He had long ago pictured to himself a future with Sónya, and that was all clear and simple just because it had all been thought out and he knew all there was in Sónya, but it was impossible to picture a future with Princess Mary, because he did not understand her but simply loved her.

Reveries about Sónya had had something merry and playful in them, but to dream of Princess Mary was always difficult and a little frightening.

"How she prayed!" he thought. "It was plain that her whole soul was in her prayer. Yes, that was the prayer that moves mountains, and I am sure her prayer will be answered. Why don't I pray for what I want?" he suddenly thought. "What do I want? To be free, released from Sónya... She was right," he thought, remembering what the governor's wife had said: "Nothing but misfortune can come of marrying Sónya. Muddles, grief for Mamma... business difficulties... muddles, terrible muddles! Besides, I don't love her—not as I should. O, God! release me from this dreadful, inextricable position!" he suddenly began to pray. "Yes, prayer can move mountains, but one must have faith and not pray as Natásha and I used to as children, that the snow might turn into sugar—and then run out into the yard to see whether it had done so. No, but I am not praying for trifles now," he thought as he put his pipe down in a corner, and folding his hands placed himself before the icon. Softened by memories of Princess Mary he began to pray as he had not done for a long time. Tears were in his eyes and in his throat when the door opened and Lavrúshka came in with some papers.

"Blockhead! Why do you come in without being called?" cried Nicholas, quickly changing his attitude.

"From the governor," said Lavrúshka in a sleepy voice. "A courier has arrived and there's a letter for you."

"Well, all right, thanks. You can go!"

Nicholas took the two letters, one of which was from his mother and the other from Sónya. He recognized them by the handwriting and opened Sónya's first. He had read only a few lines when he turned pale and his eyes opened wide with fear and joy.

"No, it's not possible!" he cried aloud.

Unable to sit still he paced up and down the room holding the letter and reading it. He glanced through it, then read it again, and then again, and standing still in the middle of the room he raised his shoulders, stretching out his hands, with his mouth wide open and his eyes fixed. What he had just been praying for with confidence that God would hear him had come to pass; but Nicholas was as much astonished as if it were something extraordinary and unexpected, and as if the very fact that it had happened so quickly proved that it had not come from God to whom he had prayed, but by some ordinary coincidence.

This unexpected and, as it seemed to Nicholas, quite voluntary letter from Sónya freed him from the knot that fettered him and from which there had seemed no escape. She wrote that the last unfortunate events—the loss of almost the whole of the Rostóvs' Moscow property—and the countess' repeatedly expressed wish that Nicholas should marry Princess Bolkónskaya, together with his silence and coldness of late, had all combined to make her decide to release him from his promise and set him completely free.

It would be too painful to me to think that I might be a cause of sorrow or discord in the family that has been so good to me (she wrote), and my love has no aim but the happiness of those I love; so, Nicholas, I beg you to consider yourself free, and to be assured that, in spite of everything, no one can love you more than does

Your Sónya

Both letters were written from Tróitsa. The other, from the countess, described their last days in Moscow, their departure, the fire, and the destruction of all their property. In this letter the countess also mentioned that Prince Andrew was among the wounded traveling with them; his state was very critical, but the doctor said there was now more hope. Sónya and Natásha were nursing him.

Next day Nicholas took his mother's letter and went to see Princess Mary. Neither he nor she said a word about what "Natásha nursing him" might mean, but thanks to this letter Nicholas suddenly became almost as intimate with the princess as if they were relations.

The following day he saw Princess Mary off on her journey to Yaroslávl, and a few days later left to rejoin his regiment.

CHAPTER VIII

S ónya's letter written from Tróitsa, which had come as an answer to Nicholas' prayer, was prompted by this: the thought of getting Nicholas married to an heiress occupied the old countess' mind more and more. She knew that Sónya was the chief obstacle to this happening, and Sónya's life in the countess' house had grown harder and harder, especially after they had received a letter from Nicholas telling of his meeting with Princess Mary in Boguchárovo. The countess let no occasion slip of making humiliating or cruel allusions to Sónya.

But a few days before they left Moscow, moved and excited by all that was going on, she called Sónya to her and, instead of reproaching and making demands on her, tearfully implored her to sacrifice herself and repay all that the family had done for her by breaking off her engagement with Nicholas.

"I shall not be at peace till you promise me this."

Sónya burst into hysterical tears and replied through her sobs that she would do anything and was prepared for anything, but gave no actual promise and could not bring herself to decide to do what was demanded of her. She must sacrifice herself for the family that had reared and brought her up. To sacrifice herself for others was Sónya's habit. Her position in the house was such that only by sacrifice could she show her worth, and she was accustomed to this and loved doing it. But in all her former acts of self-sacrifice she had been happily conscious that they raised her in her own esteem and in that of others, and so made her more worthy of Nicholas whom she loved more than anything in the world. But now they wanted her to sacrifice the very thing that constituted the whole reward for her self-sacrifice and the whole meaning of her life. And for the first time she felt bitterness against those who had been her benefactors only to torture her the more painfully; she felt jealous of Natásha who had never experienced anything of this sort, had never needed to sacrifice herself, but made others sacrifice themselves for her and yet was beloved by everybody. And for the first time Sónya felt that out of her pure, quiet love for Nicholas a passionate feeling was beginning to grow up which was stronger than principle, virtue, or religion. Under the influence of this feeling Sónya, whose life of dependence had taught her involuntarily to be secretive, having answered the countess in vague general terms, avoided talking with her and resolved to wait till she should see Nicholas, not in order to set him free but on the contrary at that meeting to bind him to her forever.

The bustle and terror of the Rostóvs' last days in Moscow stifled the gloomy thoughts that oppressed Sónya. She was glad to find escape from them in practical activity. But when she heard of Prince Andrew's presence in their house, despite her sincere pity for him and for Natásha, she was seized by a joyful and superstitious feeling that God did not intend her to be separated from Nicholas. She knew that Natásha loved no one but Prince Andrew and had never ceased to love him. She knew that being thrown together again under such terrible circumstances they would again fall in love with one another, and that Nicholas would then not be able to marry Princess Mary as they would be within the prohibited degrees of affinity. Despite all the terror of what had happened during those last days and during the first days of their journey, this feeling that Providence was intervening in her personal affairs cheered Sónya.

At the Tróitsa monastery the Rostóvs first broke their journey for a whole day.

Three large rooms were assigned to them in the monastery hostelry, one of which was occupied by Prince Andrew. The wounded man was much better that day and Natásha was sitting with him. In the next room sat the count and countess respectfully conversing with the prior, who was calling on them as old acquaintances and benefactors of the monastery. Sónya was there too, tormented by curiosity as to what Prince Andrew and Natásha were talking about.

She heard the sound of their voices through the door. That door opened and Natásha came out, looking excited. Not noticing the monk, who had risen to greet her and was drawing back the wide sleeve on his right arm, she went up to Sónya and took her hand.

"Natásha, what are you about? Come here!" said the countess.

Natásha went up to the monk for his blessing, and he advised her to pray for aid to God and His saint.

As soon as the prior withdrew, Natásha took her friend by the hand and went with her into the unoccupied room.

"Sónya, will he live?" she asked. "Sónya, how happy I am, and how unhappy!... Sónya, dovey, everything is as it used to be. If only he lives! He cannot... because... because... of..." and Natásha burst into tears.

"Yes! I knew it! Thank God!" murmured Sónya. "He will live."

Sónya was not less agitated than her friend by the latter's fear and grief and by her own personal feelings which she shared with no one. Sobbing, she kissed and comforted Natásha. "If only he lives!" she thought. Having wept, talked, and wiped away their tears, the two friends went together to Prince Andrew's door. Natásha opened it cautiously and glanced into the room, Sónya standing beside her at the half-open door.

Prince Andrew was lying raised high on three pillows. His pale face was calm, his eyes closed, and they could see his regular breathing.

"O, Natásha!" Sónya suddenly almost screamed, catching her companion's arm and stepping back from the door.

"What? What is it?" asked Natásha.

"It's that, that..." said Sónya, with a white face and trembling lips.

Natásha softly closed the door and went with Sónya to the window, not yet understanding what the latter was telling her.

"You remember," said Sónya with a solemn and frightened expression. "You remember when I looked in the mirror for you... at Otrádnoe at Christmas? Do you remember what I saw?"

"Yes, yes!" cried Natásha opening her eyes wide, and vaguely recalling that Sónya had told her something about Prince Andrew whom she had seen lying down.

"You remember?" Sónya went on. "I saw it then and told everybody, you and Dunyásha. I saw him lying on a bed," said she, making a gesture with her hand and a lifted finger at each detail, "and that he had his eyes closed and was covered just with a pink quilt, and that his hands were folded," she concluded, convincing herself that the details she had just seen were exactly what she had seen in the mirror.

She had in fact seen nothing then but had mentioned the first thing that came into her head, but what she had invented then seemed to her now as real as any other recollection. She not only remembered what she had then said—that he turned to look at her and smiled and was covered with something red—but was firmly convinced that she had then seen and said that he was covered with a pink quilt and that his eyes were closed.

"Yes, yes, it really was pink!" cried Natásha, who now thought she too remembered the word pink being used, and saw in this the most extraordinary and mysterious part of the prediction.

"But what does it mean?" she added meditatively.

"Oh, I don't know, it is all so strange," replied Sónya, clutching at her head.

A few minutes later Prince Andrew rang and Natásha went to him, but Sónya, feeling unusually excited and touched, remained at the window thinking about the strangeness of what had occurred.

They had an opportunity that day to send letters to the army, and the countess was writing to her son.

"Sónya!" said the countess, raising her eyes from her letter as her niece passed, "Sónya, won't you write to Nicholas?" She spoke in a soft, tremulous voice, and in the weary eyes that looked over her spectacles Sónya read all that the countess meant to convey with these words. Those eyes expressed entreaty, shame at having to ask, fear of a refusal, and readiness for relentless hatred in case of such refusal.

Sónya went up to the countess and, kneeling down, kissed her hand.

"Yes, Mamma, I will write," said she.

Sónya was softened, excited, and touched by all that had occurred that day, especially by the mysterious fulfillment she had just seen of her vision. Now that she knew that the renewal of Natásha's relations with Prince Andrew would prevent Nicholas from marrying Princess Mary, she was joyfully conscious of a return of that self-sacrificing spirit in which she was accustomed to live and loved to live. So with a joyful consciousness of performing a magnanimous deed— interrupted several times by the tears that dimmed her velvety black eyes—she wrote that touching letter the arrival of which had so amazed Nicholas.

CHAPTER IX

The officer and soldiers who had arrested Pierre treated him with hostility but yet with respect, in the guardhouse to which he was taken. In their attitude toward him could still be felt both uncertainty as to who he might be—perhaps a very important person—and hostility as a result of their recent personal conflict with him.

But when the guard was relieved next morning, Pierre felt that for the new guard—both officers and men—he was not as interesting as he had been to his captors; and in fact the guard of the second day did not recognize in this big, stout man in a peasant coat the vigorous person who had fought so desperately with the marauder and the convoy and had uttered those solemn words about saving a child; they saw in him only No. 17 of the captured Russians, arrested and detained for some reason by order of the Higher Command. If they noticed anything remarkable about Pierre, it was only his unabashed, meditative concentration and thoughtfulness, and the way he spoke French, which struck them as surprisingly good. In spite of this he was placed that day with the other arrested suspects, as the separate room he had occupied was required by an officer.

All the Russians confined with Pierre were men of the lowest class and, recognizing him as a gentleman, they all avoided him, more especially as he spoke French. Pierre felt sad at hearing them making fun of him.

That evening he learned that all these prisoners (he, probably, among them) were to be tried for incendiarism. On the third day he was taken with the others to a house where a French general with a white mustache sat with two colonels and other Frenchmen with scarves on their arms. With the precision and definiteness customary in addressing prisoners, and which is supposed to preclude human frailty, Pierre like the others was questioned as to who he was, where he had been, with what object, and so on.

These questions, like questions put at trials generally, left the essence of the matter aside, shut out the possibility of that essence's being revealed, and were designed only to form a channel through which the judges wished the answers of the accused to flow so as to lead to the desired result, namely a conviction. As soon as Pierre began to say anything that did not fit in with that aim, the channel was removed and the water could flow to waste. Pierre felt, moreover, what the accused always feel at their trial, perplexity as to why these questions were put to him. He had a feeling that it was only out of condescension or a kind of civility that this device of placing a channel was employed. He knew he was in these men's power, that only by force had they brought him there, that force alone gave them the right to demand answers to their questions, and that the sole object of that assembly was to inculpate him. And so, as they had the power and wish to inculpate him, this expedient of an inquiry and trial seemed unnecessary. It was evident that any answer would lead to conviction. When asked what he was doing when he was arrested, Pierre replied in a rather tragic manner that he was restoring to its parents a child he had saved from the flames. Why had he fought the marauder? Pierre answered that he "was protecting a woman," and that "to protect a woman who was being insulted was the duty of every man; that..." They interrupted him, for this was not to the point. Why was he in the yard of a burning house where witnesses had seen him? He replied that he had gone out to see what was happening in Moscow. Again they interrupted him: they had not asked where he was going, but why he was found near the fire? Who was he? they asked, repeating their first question, which he had declined to answer. Again he replied that he could not answer it.

"Put that down, that's bad... very bad," sternly remarked the general with the white mustache and red flushed face.

On the fourth day fires broke out on the Zúbovski rampart.

Pierre and thirteen others were moved to the coach house of a merchant's house near the Crimean bridge. On his way through the streets Pierre felt stifled by the smoke which seemed to hang over the whole city. Fires were visible on all sides. He did not then realize the significance of the burning of Moscow, and looked at the fires with horror.

He passed four days in the coach house near the Crimean bridge and during that time learned, from the talk of the French soldiers, that all those confined there were awaiting a decision which might come any day from the marshal. What marshal this was, Pierre could not learn from the soldiers. Evidently for them "the marshal" represented a very high and rather mysterious power.

These first days, before the eighth of September when the prisoners were had up for a second examination, were the hardest of all for Pierre.

CHAPTER X

On the eighth of September an officer—a very important one judging by the respect the guards showed him—entered the coach house where the prisoners were. This officer, probably someone on the staff, was holding a paper in his hand, and called over all the Russians there, naming Pierre as "the man who does not give his name." Glancing indolently and indifferently at all the prisoners, he ordered the officer in charge to have them decently dressed and tidied up before taking them to the marshal. An hour later a squad of soldiers arrived and Pierre with thirteen others was led to the Virgin's Field. It was a fine day, sunny after rain, and the air was unusually pure. The smoke did not hang low as on the day when Pierre had been taken from the guardhouse on the Zúbovski rampart, but rose through the pure air in columns. No flames were seen, but columns of smoke rose on all sides, and all Moscow as far as Pierre could see was one vast charred ruin. On all sides there were waste spaces with only stoves and chimney stacks still standing, and here and there the blackened walls of some brick houses. Pierre gazed at the ruins and did not recognize districts he had known well. Here and there he could see churches that had not been burned. The Krémlin, which was not destroyed, gleamed white in the distance with its towers and the belfry of Iván the Great. The domes of the New Convent of the Virgin glittered brightly and its bells were ringing particularly clearly. These bells reminded Pierre that it was Sunday and the feast of the Nativity of the Virgin. But there seemed to be no one to celebrate this holiday: everywhere were blackened ruins, and the few Russians to be seen were tattered and frightened people who tried to hide when they saw the French.

It was plain that the Russian nest was ruined and destroyed, but in place of the Russian order of life that had been destroyed, Pierre unconsciously felt that a quite different, firm, French order had been established over this ruined nest. He felt this in the looks of the soldiers who, marching in regular ranks briskly and gaily, were escorting him and the other criminals; he felt it in the looks of an important French official in a carriage and pair driven by a soldier, whom they met on the way. He felt it in the merry sounds of regimental music he heard from the left side of the field, and felt and realized it especially from the list of prisoners the French officer had read out when he came that morning. Pierre had been taken by one set of soldiers and led first to one and then to another place with dozens of other men, and it seemed that they might have forgotten him, or confused him with the others. But no: the answers he had given when questioned had come back to him in his designation as "the man who does not give his name," and under that appellation, which to Pierre seemed terrible, they were now leading him somewhere with unhesitating assurance on their faces that he and all the other prisoners were exactly the ones they wanted and that they were being taken to the proper place. Pierre felt himself to be an insignificant chip fallen among the wheels of a machine whose action he did not understand but which was working well.

He and the other prisoners were taken to the right side of the Virgin's Field, to a large white house with an immense garden not far from the convent. This was Prince Shcherbátov's house, where Pierre had often been in other days, and which, as he learned from the talk of the soldiers, was now occupied by the marshal, the Duke of Eckmühl (Davout).

They were taken to the entrance and led into the house one by one. Pierre was the sixth to enter. He was conducted through a glass gallery, an anteroom, and a hall, which were familiar to him, into a long low study at the door of which stood an adjutant.

Davout, spectacles on nose, sat bent over a table at the further end of the room. Pierre went close up to him, but Davout, evidently consulting a paper that lay before him, did not look up. Without raising his eyes, he said in a low voice:

"Who are you?"

Pierre was silent because he was incapable of uttering a word. To him Davout was not merely a French general, but a man notorious for his cruelty. Looking at his cold face, as he sat like a stern schoolmaster who was prepared to wait awhile for an answer, Pierre felt that every instant of delay might cost him his life; but he did not know what to say. He did not venture to repeat what he had said at his first examination, yet to disclose his rank and position was dangerous and embarrassing. So he was silent. But before he had decided what to do, Davout raised his head, pushed his spectacles back on his forehead, screwed up his eyes, and looked intently at him.

"I know that man," he said in a cold, measured tone, evidently calculated to frighten Pierre.

The chill that had been running down Pierre's back now seized his head as in a vise.

"You cannot know me, General, I have never seen you..."

"He is a Russian spy," Davout interrupted, addressing another general who was present, but whom Pierre had not noticed.

Davout turned away. With an unexpected reverberation in his voice Pierre rapidly began:

"No, monseigneur," he said, suddenly remembering that Davout was a duke. "No, monseigneur, you cannot have known me. I am a militia officer and have not quitted Moscow."

"Your name?" asked Davout.

"Bezúkhov."

"What proof have I that you are not lying?"

"Monseigneur!" exclaimed Pierre, not in an offended but in a pleading voice.

Davout looked up and gazed intently at him. For some seconds they looked at one another, and that look saved Pierre. Apart from conditions of war and law, that look established human relations between the two men. At that moment an immense number of things passed dimly through both their minds, and they realized that they were both children of humanity and were brothers.

At the first glance, when Davout had only raised his head from the papers where human affairs and lives were indicated by numbers, Pierre was merely a circumstance, and Davout could have shot him without burdening his conscience with an evil deed, but now he saw in him a human being. He reflected for a moment.

"How can you show me that you are telling the truth?" said Davout coldly.

Pierre remembered Ramballe, and named him and his regiment and the street where the house was.

"You are not what you say," returned Davout.

In a trembling, faltering voice Pierre began adducing proofs of the truth of his statements.

But at that moment an adjutant entered and reported something to Davout.

Davout brightened up at the news the adjutant brought, and began buttoning up his uniform. It seemed that he had quite forgotten Pierre.

When the adjutant reminded him of the prisoner, he jerked his head in Pierre's direction with a frown and ordered him to be led away. But where they were to take him Pierre did not know: back to the coach house or to the place of execution his companions had pointed out to him as they crossed the Virgin's Field.

He turned his head and saw that the adjutant was putting another question to Davout.

"Yes, of course!" replied Davout, but what this "yes" meant, Pierre did not know.

Pierre could not afterwards remember how he went, whether it was far, or in which direction. His faculties were quite numbed, he was stupefied, and noticing nothing around him went on moving his legs as the others did till they all stopped and he stopped too. The only thought in his mind at that time was: who was it that had really sentenced him to death? Not the men on the commission that had first examined him—not one of them wished to or, evidently, could have done it. It was not Davout, who had looked at him in so human a way. In another moment Davout would have realized that he was doing wrong, but just then the adjutant had come in and interrupted him. The adjutant, also, had evidently had no evil intent though he might have refrained from coming in. Then who was executing him, killing him, depriving him of life—him, Pierre, with all his memories, aspirations, hopes, and thoughts? Who was doing this? And Pierre felt that it was no one.

It was a system—a concurrence of circumstances.

A system of some sort was killing him—Pierre—depriving him of life, of everything, annihilating him.

CHAPTER XI

From Prince Shcherbátov's house the prisoners were led straight down the Virgin's Field, to the left of the nunnery, as far as a kitchen garden in which a post had been set up. Beyond that post a fresh pit had been dug in the ground, and near the post and the pit a large crowd stood in a semicircle. The crowd consisted of a few Russians and many of Napoleon's soldiers who were not on duty—Germans, Italians, and Frenchmen, in a variety of uniforms. To the right and left of the post stood rows of French troops in blue uniforms with red epaulets and high boots and shakos.

The prisoners were placed in a certain order, according to the list (Pierre was sixth), and were led to the post. Several drums suddenly began to beat on both sides of them, and at that sound Pierre felt as if part of his soul had been torn away. He lost the power of thinking or understanding. He could only hear and see. And he had only one wish—that the frightful thing that had to happen should happen quickly. Pierre looked round at his fellow prisoners and scrutinized them.

The two first were convicts with shaven heads. One was tall and thin, the other dark, shaggy, and sinewy, with a flat nose. The third was a domestic serf, about forty-five years old, with grizzled hair and a plump, well-nourished body. The fourth was a peasant, a very handsome man with a broad, light-brown beard and black eyes. The fifth was a factory hand, a thin, sallow-faced lad of eighteen in a loose coat.

Pierre heard the French consulting whether to shoot them separately or two at a time. "In couples," replied the officer in command in a calm voice. There was a stir in the ranks of the soldiers and it was evident that they were all hurrying—not as men hurry to do something they understand, but as people hurry to finish a necessary but unpleasant and incomprehensible task.

A French official wearing a scarf came up to the right of the row of prisoners and read out the sentence in Russian and in French.

Then two pairs of Frenchmen approached the criminals and at the officer's command took the two convicts who stood first in the row. The convicts stopped when they reached the post and, while sacks were being brought, looked dumbly around as a wounded beast looks at an approaching huntsman. One crossed himself continually, the other scratched his back and made a movement of the lips resembling a smile. With hurried hands the soldiers blindfolded them, drawing the sacks over their heads, and bound them to the post.

Twelve sharpshooters with muskets stepped out of the ranks with a firm regular tread and halted eight paces from the post. Pierre turned away to avoid seeing what was going to happen. Suddenly a crackling, rolling noise was heard which seemed to him louder than the most terrific thunder, and he looked round. There was some smoke, and the Frenchmen were doing something near the pit, with pale faces and trembling hands. Two more prisoners were led up. In the same way and with similar looks, these two glanced vainly at the onlookers with only a silent appeal for protection in their eyes, evidently unable to understand or believe what was going to happen to them. They could not believe it because they alone knew what their life meant to them, and so they neither understood nor believed that it could be taken from them.

Again Pierre did not wish to look and again turned away; but again the sound as of a frightful explosion struck his ear, and at the same moment he saw smoke, blood, and the pale, scared faces of the Frenchmen who were again doing something by the post, their trembling hands impeding one another. Pierre, breathing heavily, looked around as if asking what it meant. The same question was expressed in all the looks that met his.

On the faces of all the Russians and of the French soldiers and officers without exception, he read the same dismay, horror, and conflict that were in his own heart. "But who, after all, is doing this? They are all suffering as I am. Who then is it? Who?" flashed for an instant through his mind.

"Sharpshooters of the 86th, forward!" shouted someone. The fifth prisoner, the one next to Pierre, was led away—alone. Pierre did not understand that he was saved, that he and the rest had been brought there only to witness the execution. With ever-growing horror, and no sense of joy or relief, he gazed at what was taking place. The fifth man was the factory lad in the loose cloak. The moment they laid hands on him he sprang aside in terror and clutched at Pierre. (Pierre shuddered and shook himself free.) The lad was unable to walk. They dragged him along, holding him up under the arms, and he screamed. When they got him to the post he grew quiet, as if he suddenly understood something. Whether he understood that screaming was useless or whether he thought it incredible that men should kill him, at any rate he took his stand at the post, waiting to be blindfolded like the others, and like a wounded animal looked around him with glittering eyes.

Pierre was no longer able to turn away and close his eyes. His curiosity and agitation, like that of the whole crowd, reached the highest pitch at this fifth murder. Like the others this fifth man seemed calm; he wrapped his loose cloak closer and rubbed one bare foot with the other.

When they began to blindfold him he himself adjusted the knot which hurt the back of his head; then when they propped him against the bloodstained post, he leaned back and, not being comfortable in that position, straightened himself, adjusted his feet, and leaned back again more comfortably. Pierre did not take his eyes from him and did not miss his slightest movement.

Probably a word of command was given and was followed by the reports of eight muskets; but try as he would Pierre could not afterwards remember having heard the slightest sound of the shots. He only saw how the workman suddenly sank down on the cords that held him, how blood showed itself in two places, how the ropes slackened under the weight of the hanging body, and how the workman sat down, his head hanging unnaturally and one leg bent under him. Pierre ran up to the post. No one hindered him. Pale, frightened people were doing something around the workman. The lower jaw of an old Frenchman with a thick mustache trembled as he untied the ropes. The body collapsed. The soldiers dragged it awkwardly from the post and began pushing it into the pit.

They all plainly and certainly knew that they were criminals who must hide the traces of their guilt as quickly as possible.

Pierre glanced into the pit and saw that the factory lad was lying with his knees close up to his head and one shoulder higher than the other. That shoulder rose and fell rhythmically and convulsively, but spadefuls of earth were already being thrown over the whole body. One of the soldiers, evidently suffering, shouted gruffly and angrily at Pierre to go back. But Pierre did not understand him and remained near the post, and no one drove him away.

When the pit had been filled up a command was given. Pierre was taken back to his place, and the rows of troops on both sides of the post made a half turn and went past it at a measured pace. The twenty-four sharpshooters with discharged muskets, standing in the center of the circle, ran back to their places as the companies passed by.

Pierre gazed now with dazed eyes at these sharpshooters who ran in couples out of the circle. All but one rejoined their companies. This one, a young soldier, his face deadly pale, his shako pushed back, and his musket resting on the ground, still stood near the pit at the spot from which he had fired. He swayed like a drunken man, taking some steps forward and back to save himself from falling. An old, noncommissioned officer ran out of the ranks and taking him by the elbow dragged him to his company. The crowd of Russians and Frenchmen began to disperse. They all went away silently and with drooping heads.

"That will teach them to start fires," said one of the Frenchmen.

Pierre glanced round at the speaker and saw that it was a soldier who was trying to find some relief after what had been done, but was not able to do so. Without finishing what he had begun to say he made a hopeless movement with his arm and went away.

CHAPTER XII

After the execution Pierre was separated from the rest of the prisoners and placed alone in a small, ruined, and befouled church.

Toward evening a noncommissioned officer entered with two soldiers and told him that he had been pardoned and would now go to the barracks for the prisoners of war. Without understanding what was said to him, Pierre got up and went with the soldiers. They took him to the upper end of the field, where there were some sheds built of charred planks, beams, and battens, and led him into one of them. In the darkness some twenty different men surrounded Pierre. He looked at them without understanding who they were, why they were there, or what they wanted of him. He heard what they said, but did not understand the meaning of the words and made no kind of deduction from or application of them. He replied to questions they put to him, but did not consider who was listening to his replies, nor how they would understand them. He looked at their faces and figures, but they all seemed to him equally meaningless.

From the moment Pierre had witnessed those terrible murders committed by men who did not wish to commit them, it was as if the mainspring of his life, on which everything depended and which made everything appear alive, had suddenly been wrenched out and everything had collapsed into a heap of meaningless rubbish. Though he did not acknowledge it to himself, his faith in the right ordering of the universe, in humanity, in his own soul, and in God, had been destroyed. He had experienced this before, but never so strongly as now. When similar doubts had assailed him before, they had been the result of his own wrongdoing, and at the bottom of his heart he had felt that relief from his despair and from those doubts was to be found within himself. But now he felt that the universe had crumbled before his eyes and only meaningless ruins remained, and this not by any fault of his own. He felt that it was not in his power to regain faith in the meaning of life.

Around him in the darkness men were standing and evidently something about him interested them greatly. They were telling him something and asking him something. Then they led him away somewhere, and at last he found himself in a corner of the shed among men who were laughing and talking on all sides.

"Well, then, mates... that very prince *who*..." some voice at the other end of the shed was saying, with a strong emphasis on the word *who*.

Sitting silent and motionless on a heap of straw against the wall, Pierre sometimes opened and sometimes closed his eyes. But as soon as he closed them he saw before him the dreadful face of the factory lad—especially dreadful because of its simplicity—and the faces of the murderers, even more dreadful because of their disquiet. And he opened his eyes again and stared vacantly into the darkness around him.

Beside him in a stooping position sat a small man of whose presence he was first made aware by a strong smell of perspiration which came from him every time he moved. This man was doing something to his legs in the darkness, and though Pierre could not see his face he felt that the man continually glanced at him. On growing used to the darkness Pierre saw that the man was taking off his leg bands, and the way he did it aroused Pierre's interest.

Having unwound the string that tied the band on one leg, he carefully coiled it up and immediately set to work on the other leg, glancing up at Pierre. While one hand hung up the first string the other was already unwinding the band on the second leg. In this way, having carefully removed the leg bands by deft circular motions of his arm following one another uninterruptedly, the man hung the leg bands up on some pegs fixed above his head. Then he took out a knife, cut something, closed the knife, placed it under the head of his bed, and, seating himself comfortably, clasped his arms round his lifted knees and fixed his eyes on Pierre. The latter was conscious of something pleasant, comforting, and well-rounded in these deft movements, in the man's well-ordered arrangements in his corner, and even in his very smell, and he looked at the man without taking his eyes from him.

"You've seen a lot of trouble, sir, eh?" the little man suddenly said.

And there was so much kindliness and simplicity in his singsong voice that Pierre tried to reply, but his jaw trembled and he felt tears rising to his eyes. The little fellow, giving Pierre no time to betray his confusion, instantly continued in the same pleasant tones:

"Eh, lad, don't fret!" said he, in the tender singsong caressing voice old Russian peasant women employ. "Don't fret, friend—'suffer an hour, live for an age!' that's how it is, my dear fellow. And here we live, thank heaven, without offense. Among these folk, too, there are good men as well as bad," said he, and still speaking, he turned on his knees with a supple movement, got up, coughed, and went off to another part of the shed.

"Eh, you rascal!" Pierre heard the same kind voice saying at the other end of the shed. "So you've come, you rascal? She remembers... Now, now, that'll do!"

And the soldier, pushing away a little dog that was jumping up at him, returned to his place and sat down. In his hands he had something wrapped in a rag.

"Here, eat a bit, sir," said he, resuming his former respectful tone as he unwrapped and offered Pierre some baked potatoes. "We had soup for dinner and the potatoes are grand!"

Pierre had not eaten all day and the smell of the potatoes seemed extremely pleasant to him. He thanked the soldier and began to eat.

"Well, are they all right?" said the soldier with a smile. "You should do like this."

He took a potato, drew out his clasp knife, cut the potato into two equal halves on the palm of his hand, sprinkled some salt on it from the rag, and handed it to Pierre.

"The potatoes are grand!" he said once more. "Eat some like that!"

Pierre thought he had never eaten anything that tasted better.

"Oh, I'm all right," said he, "but why did they shoot those poor fellows? The last one was hardly twenty."

"Tss, tt...!" said the little man. "Ah, what a sin... what a sin!" he added quickly, and as if his words were always waiting ready in his mouth and flew out involuntarily he went on: "How was it, sir, that you stayed in Moscow?"

"I didn't think they would come so soon. I stayed accidentally," replied Pierre.

"And how did they arrest you, dear lad? At your house?"

"No, I went to look at the fire, and they arrested me there, and tried me as an incendiary."

"Where there's law there's injustice," put in the little man.

"And have you been here long?" Pierre asked as he munched the last of the potato.

"I? It was last Sunday they took me, out of a hospital in Moscow."

"Why, are you a soldier then?"

"Yes, we are soldiers of the Ápsheron regiment. I was dying of fever. We weren't told anything. There were some twenty of us lying there. We had no idea, never guessed at all."

"And do you feel sad here?" Pierre inquired.

"How can one help it, lad? My name is Platón, and the surname is Karatáev," he added, evidently wishing to make it easier for Pierre to address him. "They call me 'little falcon' in the regiment. How is one to help feeling sad? Moscow—she's the mother of cities. How can one see all this and not feel sad? But 'the maggot gnaws the cabbage, yet dies first'; that's what the old folks used to tell us," he added rapidly.

"What? What did you say?" asked Pierre.

"Who? I?" said Karatáev. "I say things happen not as we plan but as God judges," he replied, thinking that he was repeating what he had said before, and immediately continued:

"Well, and you, have you a family estate, sir? And a house? So you have abundance, then? And a housewife? And your old parents, are they still living?" he asked.

And though it was too dark for Pierre to see, he felt that a suppressed smile of kindliness puckered the soldier's lips as he put these questions. He seemed grieved that Pierre had no parents, especially that he had no mother.

"A wife for counsel, a mother-in-law for welcome, but there's none as dear as one's own mother!" said he. "Well, and have you little ones?" he went on asking.

Again Pierre's negative answer seemed to distress him, and he hastened to add:

"Never mind! You're young folks yet, and please God may still have some. The great thing is to live in harmony...."

"But it's all the same now," Pierre could not help saying.

"Ah, my dear fellow!" rejoinedKarataév, "never decline a prison or a beggar's sack!"

He seated himself more comfortably and coughed, evidently preparing to tell a long story.

"Well, my dear fellow, I was still living at home," he began. "We had a well-to-do homestead, plenty of land, we peasants lived well and our house was one to thank God for. When Father and we went out mowing there were seven of us. We lived well. We were real peasants. It so happened..."

And PlatónKarataév told a long story of how he had gone into someone's copse to take wood, how he had been caught by the keeper, had been tried, flogged, and sent to serve as a soldier.

"Well, lad," and a smile changed the tone of his voice, "we thought it was a misfortune but it turned out a blessing! If it had not been for my sin, my brother would have had to go as a soldier. But he, my younger brother, had five little ones, while I, you see, only left a wife behind. We had a little girl, but God took her before I went as a soldier. I come home on leave and I'll tell you how it was, I look and see that they are living better than before. The yard full of cattle, the women at home, two brothers away earning wages, and only Michael the youngest, at home. Father, he says, 'All my children are the same to me: it hurts the same whichever finger gets bitten. But if Platón hadn't been shaved for a soldier, Michael would have had to go.' called us all to him and, will you believe it, placed us in front of the icons. 'Michael,' he says, 'come here and bow down to his feet; and you, young woman, you bow down too; and you, grandchildren, also bow down before him! Do you understand?' he says. That's how it is, dear fellow. Fate looks for a head. But we are always judging, 'that's not well—that's not right!' Our luck is like water in a dragnet: you pull at it and it bulges, but when you've drawn it out it's empty! That's how it is."

And Platón shifted his seat on the straw.

After a short silence he rose.

"Well, I think you must be sleepy," said he, and began rapidly crossing himself and repeating:

"Lord Jesus Christ, holy Saint Nicholas, Frola and Lavra! Lord Jesus Christ, holy Saint Nicholas, Frola and Lavra! Lord Jesus Christ, have mercy on us and save us!" he concluded, then bowed to the ground, got up, sighed, and sat down again on his heap of straw. "That's the way. Lay me down like a stone, O God, and raise me up like a loaf," he muttered as he lay down, pulling his coat over him.

"What prayer was that you were saying?" asked Pierre.

"Eh?" murmured Platón, who had almost fallen asleep. "What was I saying? I was praying. Don't you pray?"

"Yes, I do," said Pierre. "But what was that you said: Frola and Lavra?"

"Well, of course," replied Platón quickly, "the horses' saints. One must pity the animals too. Eh, the rascal! Now you've curled up and got warm, you daughter of a bitch!" said Karatáev, touching the dog that lay at his feet, and again turning over he fell asleep immediately.

Sounds of crying and screaming came from somewhere in the distance outside, and flames were visible through the cracks of the shed, but inside it was quiet and dark. For a long time Pierre did not sleep, but lay with eyes open in the darkness, listening to the regular snoring of Platón who lay beside him, and he felt that the world that had been shattered was once more stirring in his soul with a new beauty and on new and unshakable foundations.

CHAPTER XIII

Twenty-three soldiers, three officers, and two officials were confined in the shed in which Pierre had been placed and where he remained for four weeks.

When Pierre remembered them afterwards they all seemed misty figures to him except PlatónKaratáev, who always remained in his mind a most vivid and precious memory and the personification of everything Russian, kindly, and round. When Pierre saw his neighbor next morning at dawn the first impression of him, as of something round, was fully confirmed: Platón's whole figure—in a French overcoat girdled with a cord, a soldier's cap, and bast shoes—was round. His head was quite round, his back, chest, shoulders, and even his arms, which he held as if ever ready to embrace something, were rounded, his pleasant smile and his large, gentle brown eyes were also round.

PlatónKaratáev must have been fifty, judging by his stories of campaigns he had been in, told as by an old soldier. He did not himself know his age and was quite unable to determine it. But his brilliantly white, strong teeth which showed in two unbroken semicircles when he laughed—as he often did—were all sound and good, there was not a gray hair in his beard or on his head, and his whole body gave an impression of suppleness and especially of firmness and endurance.

His face, despite its fine, rounded wrinkles, had an expression of innocence and youth, his voice was pleasant and musical. But the chief peculiarity of his speech was its directness and appositeness. It was evident that he never considered what he had said or was going to say, and consequently the rapidity and justice of his intonation had an irresistible persuasiveness.

His physical strength and agility during the first days of his imprisonment were such that he seemed not to know what fatigue and sickness meant. Every night before lying down, he said: "Lord, lay me down as a stone and raise me up as a loaf!" and every morning on getting up, he said: "I lay down and curled up, I get up and shake myself." And indeed he only had to lie down, to fall asleep like a stone, and he only had to shake himself, to be ready without a moment's delay for some work, just as children are ready to play directly they awake. He could do everything, not very well but not badly. He baked, cooked, sewed, planed, and mended boots. He was always busy, and only at night allowed himself conversation—of which he was fond—and songs. He did not sing like a trained singer who knows he is listened to, but like the birds, evidently giving vent to the sounds in the same way that one stretches oneself or walks about to get rid of stiffness, and the sounds were always high-pitched, mournful, delicate, and almost feminine, and his face at such times was very serious.

Having been taken prisoner and allowed his beard to grow, he seemed to have thrown off all that had been forced upon him— everything military and alien to himself—and had returned to his former peasant habits.

"A soldier on leave—a shirt outside breeches," he would say.

He did not like talking about his life as a soldier, though he did not complain, and often mentioned that he had not been flogged once during the whole of his army service. When he related anything it was generally some old and evidently precious memory of his "Christian" life, as he called his peasant existence. The proverbs, of which his talk was full, were for the most part not the coarse and indecent saws soldiers employ, but those folk sayings which taken without a context seem so insignificant, but when used appositely suddenly acquire a significance of profound wisdom.

He would often say the exact opposite of what he had said on a previous occasion, yet both would be right. He liked to talk and he talked well, adorning his speech with terms of endearment and with folk sayings which Pierre thought he invented himself, but the chief charm of his talk lay in the fact that the commonest events—

sometimes just such as Pierre had witnessed without taking notice of them—assumed in Karatáev's a character of solemn fitness. He liked to hear the folk tales one of the soldiers used to tell of an evening (they were always the same), but most of all he liked to hear stories of real life. He would smile joyfully when listening to such stories, now and then putting in a word or asking a question to make the moral beauty of what he was told clear to himself. Karatáev had no attachments, friendships, or love, as Pierre understood them, but loved and lived affectionately with everything life brought him in contact with, particularly with man—not any particular man, but those with whom he happened to be. He loved his dog, his comrades, the French, and Pierre who was his neighbor, but Pierre felt that in spite of Karatáev's affectionate tenderness for him (by which he unconsciously gave Pierre's spiritual life its due) he would not have grieved for a moment at parting from him. And Pierre began to feel in the same way toward Karatáev.

To all the other prisoners PlatónKaratáev seemed a most ordinary soldier. They called him "little falcon" or "Platósha," chaffed him good-naturedly, and sent him on errands. But to Pierre he always remained what he had seemed that first night: an unfathomable, rounded, eternal personification of the spirit of simplicity and truth.

PlatónKaratáev knew nothing by heart except his prayers. When he began to speak he seemed not to know how he would conclude.

Sometimes Pierre, struck by the meaning of his words, would ask him to repeat them, but Platón could never recall what he had said a moment before, just as he never could repeat to Pierre the words of his favorite song: *native* and *birch tree* and *my heart is sick* occurred in it, but when spoken and not sung, no meaning could be got out of it. He did not, and could not, understand the meaning of words apart from their context. Every word and action of his was the manifestation of an activity unknown to him, which was his life. But his life, as he regarded it, had no meaning as a separate thing. It had meaning only as part of a whole of which he was always conscious. His words and actions flowed from him as evenly, inevitably, and spontaneously as fragrance exhales from a flower. He could not understand the value or significance of any word or deed taken separately.

CHAPTER XIV

When Princess Mary heard from Nicholas that her brother was with the Rostóvs at Yaroslávl she at once prepared to go there, in spite of her aunt's efforts to dissuade her—and not merely to go herself but to take her nephew with her. Whether it were difficult or easy, possible or impossible, she did not ask and did not want to know: it was her duty, not only to herself, to be near her brother who was perhaps dying, but to do everything possible to take his son to him, and so she prepared to set off. That she had not heard from Prince Andrew himself, Princess Mary attributed to his being too weak to write or to his considering the long journey too hard and too dangerous for her and his son.

In a few days Princess Mary was ready to start. Her equipages were the huge family coach in which she had traveled to Vorónezh, a semiopen trap, and a baggage cart. With her traveled Mademoiselle Bourienne, little Nicholas and his tutor, her old nurse, three maids, Tíkhon, and a young footman and courier her aunt had sent to accompany her.

The usual route through Moscow could not be thought of, and the roundabout way Princess Mary was obliged to take through Lípetsk, Ryazán, Vladímir, and Shúya was very long and, as post horses were not everywhere obtainable, very difficult, and near Ryazán where the French were said to have shown themselves was even dangerous.

During this difficult journey Mademoiselle Bourienne, Dessalles, and Princess Mary's servants were astonished at her energy and firmness of spirit. She went to bed later and rose earlier than any of them, and no difficulties daunted her. Thanks to her activity and energy, which infected her fellow travelers, they approached Yaroslávl by the end of the second week.

The last days of her stay in Vorónezh had been the happiest of her life. Her love for Rostóv no longer tormented or agitated her. It filled her whole soul, had become an integral part of herself, and she no longer struggled against it. Latterly she had become convinced that she loved and was beloved, though she never said this definitely to herself in words. She had become convinced of it at her last interview with Nicholas, when he had come to tell her that her brother was with the Rostóvs. Not by a single word had Nicholas alluded to the fact that Prince Andrew's relations with Natásha might, if he recovered, be renewed, but Princess Mary saw by his face that he knew and thought of this.

Yet in spite of that, his relation to her—considerate, delicate, and loving—not only remained unchanged, but it sometimes seemed to Princess Mary that he was even glad that the family connection between them allowed him to express his friendship more freely. She knew that she loved for the first and only time in her life and felt that she was beloved, and was happy in regard to it.

But this happiness on one side of her spiritual nature did not prevent her feeling grief for her brother with full force; on the contrary, that spiritual tranquility on the one side made it the more possible for her to give full play to her feeling for her brother. That feeling was so strong at the moment of leaving Vorónezh that those who saw her off, as they looked at her careworn, despairing face, felt sure she would fall ill on the journey. But the very difficulties and preoccupations of the journey, which she took so actively in hand, saved her for a while from her grief and gave her strength.

As always happens when traveling, Princess Mary thought only of the journey itself, forgetting its object. But as she approached Yaroslávl the thought of what might await her there—not after many days, but that very evening—again presented itself to her and her agitation increased to its utmost limit.

The courier who had been sent on in advance to find out where the Rostóvs were staying in Yaroslávl, and in what condition Prince Andrew was, when he met the big coach just entering the town gates was appalled by the terrible pallor of the princess' face that looked out at him from the window.

"I have found out everything, your excellency: the Rostóvs are staying at the merchant Brónnikov's house, in the Square not far from here, right above the Vólga," said the courier.

Princess Mary looked at him with frightened inquiry, not understanding why he did not reply to what she chiefly wanted to know: how was her brother? Mademoiselle Bourienne put that question for her.

"How is the prince?" she asked.

"His excellency is staying in the same house with them."

"Then he is alive," thought Princess Mary, and asked in a low voice: "How is he?"

"The servants say he is still the same."

What "still the same" might mean Princess Mary did not ask, but with an unnoticed glance at little seven-year-old Nicholas, who was sitting in front of her looking with pleasure at the town, she bowed her head and did not raise it again till the heavy coach, rumbling, shaking and swaying, came to a stop. The carriage steps clattered as they were let down.

The carriage door was opened. On the left there was water—a great river—and on the right a porch. There were people at the entrance: servants, and a rosy girl with a large plait of black hair, smiling as it seemed to Princess Mary in an unpleasantly affected way. (This was Sónya.) Princess Mary ran up the steps. "This way, this way!" said the girl, with the same artificial smile, and the princess found herself in the hall facing an elderly woman of Oriental type, who came rapidly to meet her with a look of emotion. This was the countess. She embraced Princess Mary and kissed her.

"*Mon enfant!*" she muttered, "*je vousaime et vousconnaisdepuislongtemps.*" *

* "My child! I love you and have known you a long time."

Despite her excitement, Princess Mary realized that this was the countess and that it was necessary to say something to her. Hardly knowing how she did it, she contrived to utter a few polite phrases in French in the same tone as those that had been addressed to her, and asked: "How is he?"

"The doctor says that he is not in danger," said the countess, but as she spoke she raised her eyes with a sigh, and her gesture conveyed a contradiction of her words.

"Where is he? Can I see him—can I?" asked the princess.

"One moment, Princess, one moment, my dear! Is this his son?" said the countess, turning to little Nicholas who was coming in with Dessalles. "There will be room for everybody, this is a big house. Oh, what a lovely boy!"

The countess took Princess Mary into the drawing room, where Sónya was talking to Mademoiselle Bourienne. The countess caressed the boy, and the old count came in and welcomed the princess. He had changed very much since Princess Mary had last seen him. Then he had been a brisk, cheerful, self-assured old man; now he seemed a pitiful, bewildered person. While talking to Princess Mary he continually looked round as if asking everyone whether he was doing the right thing. After the destruction of Moscow and of his property, thrown out of his accustomed groove he seemed to have lost the sense of his own significance and to feel that there was no longer a place for him in life.

In spite of her one desire to see her brother as soon as possible, and her vexation that at the moment when all she wanted was to see him they should be trying to entertain her and pretending to admire her nephew, the princess noticed all that was going on around her and felt the necessity of submitting, for a time, to this new order of things which she had entered. She knew it to be necessary, and though it was hard for her she was not vexed with these people.

"This is my niece," said the count, introducing Sónya—"You don't know her, Princess?"

Princess Mary turned to Sónya and, trying to stifle the hostile feeling that arose in her toward the girl, she kissed her. But she felt oppressed by the fact that the mood of everyone around her was so far from what was in her own heart.

"Where is he?" she asked again, addressing them all.

"He is downstairs. Natásha is with him," answered Sónya, flushing. "We have sent to ask. I think you must be tired, Princess."

Tears of vexation showed themselves in Princess Mary's eyes. She turned away and was about to ask the countess again how to go to him, when light, impetuous, and seemingly buoyant steps were heard at the door. The princess looked round and saw Natásha coming in, almost running—that Natáshawhom she had liked so little at their meeting in Moscow long since.

But hardly had the princess looked at Natásha's face before she realized that here was a real comrade in her grief, and consequently a friend. She ran to meet her, embraced her, and began to cry on her shoulder.

As soon as Natásha, sitting at the head of Prince Andrew's bed, heard of Princess Mary's arrival, she softly left his room and hastened to her with those swift steps that had sounded buoyant to Princess Mary.

There was only one expression on her agitated face when she ran into the drawing room—that of love—boundless love for him, for her, and for all that was near to the man she loved; and of pity, suffering for others, and passionate desire to give herself entirely to helping them. It was plain that at that moment there was in Natásha's heart no thought of herself or of her own relations with Prince Andrew.

Princess Mary, with her acute sensibility, understood all this at the first glance at Natásha's face, and wept on her shoulder with sorrowful pleasure.

"Come, come to him, Mary," said Natásha, leading her into the other room.

Princess Mary raised her head, dried her eyes, and turned to Natásha. She felt that from her she would be able to understand and learn everything.

"How..." she began her question but stopped short.

She felt that it was impossible to ask, or to answer, in words. Natásha's face and eyes would have to tell her all more clearly and profoundly.

Natásha was gazing at her, but seemed afraid and in doubt whether to say all she knew or not; she seemed to feel that before those luminous eyes which penetrated into the very depths of her heart, it was impossible not to tell the whole truth which she saw. And suddenly, Natásha's lips twitched, ugly wrinkles gathered round her mouth, and covering her face with her hands she burst into sobs.

Princess Mary understood.

But she still hoped, and asked, in words she herself did not trust:

"But how is his wound? What is his general condition?"

"You, you... will see," was all Natásha could say.

They sat a little while downstairs near his room till they had left off crying and were able to go to him with calm faces.

"How has his whole illness gone? Is it long since he grew worse? When did this happen?" Princess Mary inquired.

Natásha told her that at first there had been danger from his feverish condition and the pain he suffered, but at Tróitsa that had passed and the doctor had only been afraid of gangrene. That danger had also passed. When they reached Yaroslávl the wound had begun to fester (Natásha knew all about such things as festering) and the doctor had said that the festering might take a normal course. Then fever set in, but the doctor had said the fever was not very serious.

"But two days ago *this* suddenly happened," said Natásha, struggling with her sobs. "I don't know why, but you will see what he is like."

"Is he weaker? Thinner?" asked the princess.

"No, it's not that, but worse. You will see. O, Mary, he is too good, he cannot, cannot live, because..."

CHAPTER XV

When Natásha opened Prince Andrew's door with a familiar movement and let Princess Mary pass into the room before her, the princess felt the sobs in her throat. Hard as she had tried to prepare herself, and now tried to remain tranquil, she knew that she would be unable to look at him without tears.

The princess understood what Natásha had meant by the words: "two days ago *this* suddenly happened." She understood those words to mean that he had suddenly softened and that this softening and gentleness were signs of approaching death. As she stepped to the door she already saw in imagination Andrew's face as she remembered it in childhood, a gentle, mild, sympathetic face which he had rarely shown, and which therefore affected her very strongly. She was sure he would speak soft, tender words to her such as her father had uttered before his death, and that she would not be able to bear it and would burst into sobs in his presence. Yet sooner or later it had to be, and she went in. The sobs rose higher and higher in her throat as she more and more clearly distinguished his form and her shortsighted eyes tried to make out his features, and then she saw his face and met his gaze.

He was lying in a squirrel-fur dressing gown on a divan, surrounded by pillows. He was thin and pale. In one thin, translucently white hand he held a handkerchief, while with the other he stroked the delicate mustache he had grown, moving his fingers slowly. His eyes gazed at them as they entered.

On seeing his face and meeting his eyes Princess Mary's pace suddenly slackened, she felt her tears dry up and her sobs ceased.

She suddenly felt guilty and grew timid on catching the expression of his face and eyes.

"But in what am I to blame?" she asked herself. And his cold, stern look replied: "Because you are alive and thinking of the living, while I..."

In the deep gaze that seemed to look not outwards but inwards there was an almost hostile expression as he slowly regarded his sister and Natásha.

He kissed his sister, holding her hand in his as was their wont.

"How are you, Mary? How did you manage to get here?" said he in a voice as calm and aloof as his look.

Had he screamed in agony, that scream would not have struck such horror into Princess Mary's heart as the tone of his voice.

"And have you brought little Nicholas?" he asked in the same slow, quiet manner and with an obvious effort to remember.

"How are you now?" said Princess Mary, herself surprised at what she was saying.

"That, my dear, you must ask the doctor," he replied, and again making an evident effort to be affectionate, he said with his lips only (his words clearly did not correspond to his thoughts):

"*Merci, chère amie, d'être venue.*" *

* "Thank you for coming, my dear."

Princess Mary pressed his hand. The pressure made him wince just perceptibly. He was silent, and she did not know what to say. She now understood what had happened to him two days before. In his words, his tone, and especially in that calm, almost antagonistic look could be felt an estrangement from everything belonging to this world, terrible in one who is alive. Evidently only with an effort did he understand anything living; but it was obvious that he failed to understand, not because he lacked the power to do so but because he understood something else—something the living did not and could not understand—and which wholly occupied his mind.

"There, you see how strangely fate has brought us together," said he, breaking the silence and pointing to Natásha. "She looks after me all the time."

Princess Mary heard him and did not understand how he could say such a thing. He, the sensitive, tender Prince Andrew, how could he say that, before her whom he loved and who loved him? Had he expected to live he could not have said those words in that offensively cold tone. If he had not known that he was dying, how could he have failed to pity her and how could he speak like that in her presence? The only explanation was that he was indifferent, because something else, much more important, had been revealed to him.

The conversation was cold and disconnected and continually broke off.

"Mary came by way of Ryazán," said Natásha.

Prince Andrew did not notice that she called his sister *Mary*, and only after calling her so in his presence did Natásha notice it herself.

"Really?" he asked.

"They told her that all Moscow has been burned down, and that..."

Natásha stopped. It was impossible to talk. It was plain that he was making an effort to listen, but could not do so.

"Yes, they say it's burned," he said. "It's a great pity," and he gazed straight before him, absently stroking his mustache with his fingers.

"And so you have met Count Nicholas, Mary?" Prince Andrew suddenly said, evidently wishing to speak pleasantly to them. "He wrote here that he took a great liking to you," he went on simply and calmly, evidently unable to understand all the complex significance his words had for living people. "If you liked him too, it would be a good thing for you to get married," he added rather more quickly, as if pleased at having found words he had long been seeking.

Princess Mary heard his words but they had no meaning for her, except as a proof of how far away he now was from everything living.

"Why talk of me?" she said quietly and glanced at Natásha.

Natásha, who felt her glance, did not look at her. All three were again silent.

"Andrew, would you like..." Princess Mary suddenly said in a trembling voice, "would you like to see little Nicholas? He is always talking about you!"

Prince Andrew smiled just perceptibly and for the first time, but Princess Mary, who knew his face so well, saw with horror that he did not smile with pleasure or affection for his son, but with quiet, gentle irony because he thought she was trying what she believed to be the last means of arousing him.

"Yes, I shall be very glad to see him. Is he quite well?"

When little Nicholas was brought into Prince Andrew's room he looked at his father with frightened eyes, but did not cry, because no one else was crying. Prince Andrew kissed him and evidently did not know what to say to him.

When Nicholas had been led away, Princess Mary again went up to her brother, kissed him, and unable to restrain her tears any longer began to cry.

He looked at her attentively.

"Is it about Nicholas?" he asked.

Princess Mary nodded her head, weeping.

"Mary, you know the Gosp..." but he broke off.

"What did you say?"

"Nothing. You mustn't cry here," he said, looking at her with the same cold expression.

When Princess Mary began to cry, he understood that she was crying at the thought that little Nicholas would be left without a father. With a great effort he tried to return to life and to see things from their point of view.

"Yes, to them it must seem sad!" he thought. "But how simple it is.

"The fowls of the air sow not, neither do they reap, yet your Fatherfeedeth them," he said to himself and wished to say to Princess Mary; "but no, they will take it their own way, they won't understand! They can't understand that all those feelings they prize so—all our feelings, all those ideas that seem so important to us, are *unnecessary*. We cannot understand one another," and he remained silent.

Prince Andrew's little son was seven. He could scarcely read, and knew nothing. After that day he lived through many things, gaining knowledge, observation, and experience, but had he possessed all the faculties he afterwards acquired, he could not have had a better or more profound understanding of the meaning of the scene he had witnessed between his father, Mary, and Natásha, than he had then. He understood it completely, and, leaving the room without crying, went silently up to Natásha who had come out with him and looked shyly at her with his beautiful, thoughtful eyes, then his uplifted, rosy upper lip trembled and leaning his head against her he began to cry.

After that he avoided Dessalles and the countess who caressed him and either sat alone or came timidly to Princess Mary, or to Natásha of whom he seemed even fonder than of his aunt, and clung to them quietly and shyly.

When Princess Mary had left Prince Andrew she fully understood what Natásha's face had told her. She did not speak any more to Natásha of hopes of saving his life. She took turns with her beside his sofa, and did not cry any more, but prayed continually, turning in soul to that Eternal and Unfathomable, whose presence above the dying man was now so evident.

CHAPTER XVI

N ot only did Prince Andrew know he would die, but he felt that he was dying and was already half dead. He was conscious of an aloofness from everything earthly and a strange and joyous lightness of existence. Without haste or agitation he awaited what was coming. That inexorable, eternal, distant, and unknown the presence of which he had felt continually all his life—was now near to him and, by the strange lightness he experienced, almost comprehensible and palpable....

Formerly he had feared the end. He had twice experienced that terribly tormenting fear of death—the end—but now he no longer understood that fear.

He had felt it for the first time when the shell spun like a top before him, and he looked at the fallow field, the bushes, and the sky, and knew that he was face to face with death. When he came to himself after being wounded and the flower of eternal, unfettered love had instantly unfolded itself in his soul as if freed from the bondage of life that had restrained it, he no longer feared death and ceased to think about it.

During the hours of solitude, suffering, and partial delirium he spent after he was wounded, the more deeply he penetrated into the new principle of eternal love revealed to him, the more he unconsciously detached himself from earthly life. To love everything and everybody and always to sacrifice oneself for love meant not to love anyone, not to live this earthly life. And the more imbued he became with that principle of love, the more he renounced life and the more completely he destroyed that dreadful barrier which—in the absence of such love—stands between life and death. When during those first days he remembered that he would have to die, he said to himself: "Well, what of it? So much the better!"

But after the night in Mytíshchi when, half delirious, he had seen her for whom he longed appear before him and, having pressed her hand to his lips, had shed gentle, happy tears, love for a particular woman again crept unobserved into his heart and once more bound him to life. And joyful and agitating thoughts began to occupy his mind. Recalling the moment at the ambulance station when he had seen Kurágin, he could not now regain the feeling he then had, but was tormented by the question whether Kurágin was alive. And he dared not inquire.

His illness pursued its normal physical course, but what Natásha referred to when she said: "*This* suddenly happened," had occurred two days before Princess Mary arrived. It was the last spiritual struggle between life and death, in which death gained the victory. It was the unexpected realization of the fact that he still valued life as presented to him in the form of his love for Natásha, and a last, though ultimately vanquished, attack of terror before the unknown.

It was evening. As usual after dinner he was slightly feverish, and his thoughts were preternaturally clear. Sónya was sitting by the table. He began to doze. Suddenly a feeling of happiness seized him.

"Ah, she has come!" thought he.

And so it was: in Sónya's place sat Natásha who had just come in noiselessly.

Since she had begun looking after him, he had always experienced this physical consciousness of her nearness. She was sitting in an armchair placed sideways, screening the light of the candle from him, and was knitting a stocking. She had learned to knit stockings since Prince Andrew had casually mentioned that no one nursed the sick so well as old nurses who knit stockings, and that there is something soothing in the knitting of stockings. The needles clicked lightly in her slender, rapidly moving hands, and he could clearly see the thoughtful profile of her drooping face. She moved, and the ball rolled off her knees. She started, glanced round at him, and screening the candle with her hand stooped carefully with a supple and exact movement, picked up the ball, and regained her former position.

He looked at her without moving and saw that she wanted to draw a deep breath after stooping, but refrained from doing so and breathed cautiously.

At the Tróitsa monastery they had spoken of the past, and he had told her that if he lived he would always thank God for his wound which had brought them together again, but after that they never spoke of the future.

"Can it or can it not be?" he now thought as he looked at her and listened to the light click of the steel needles. "Can fate have brought me to her so strangely only for me to die?... Is it possible that the truth of life has been revealed to me only to show me that I have spent my life in falsity? I love her more than anything in the world! But what am I to do if I love her?" he thought, and he involuntarily groaned, from a habit acquired during his sufferings.

On hearing that sound Natásha put down the stocking, leaned nearer to him, and suddenly, noticing his shining eyes, stepped lightly up to him and bent over him.

"You are not asleep?"

"No, I have been looking at you a long time. I felt you come in. No one else gives me that sense of soft tranquillity that you do... that light. I want to weep for joy."

Natásha drew closer to him. Her face shone with rapturous joy.

"Natásha, I love you too much! More than anything in the world."

"And I!"—She turned away for an instant. "Why too much?" she asked.

"Why too much?... Well, what do you, what do you feel in your soul, your whole soul—shall I live? What do you think?"

"I am sure of it, sure!" Natásha almost shouted, taking hold of both his hands with a passionate movement.

He remained silent awhile.

"How good it would be!" and taking her hand he kissed it.

Natásha felt happy and agitated, but at once remembered that this would not do and that he had to be quiet.

"But you have not slept," she said, repressing her joy. "Try to sleep... please!"

He pressed her hand and released it, and she went back to the candle and sat down again in her former position. Twice she turned and looked at him, and her eyes met his beaming at her. She set herself a task on her stocking and resolved not to turn round till it was finished.

Soon he really shut his eyes and fell asleep. He did not sleep long and suddenly awoke with a start and in a cold perspiration.

As he fell asleep he had still been thinking of the subject that now always occupied his mind—about life and death, and chiefly about death. He felt himself nearer to it.

"Love? What is love?" he thought.

"Love hinders death. Love is life. All, everything that I understand, I understand only because I love. Everything is, everything exists, only because I love. Everything is united by it alone. Love is God, and to die means that I, a particle of love, shall return to the general and eternal source." These thoughts seemed to him comforting. But they were only thoughts. Something was lacking in them, they were not clear, they were too one-sidedly personal and brain-spun. And there was the former agitation and obscurity. He fell asleep.

He dreamed that he was lying in the room he really was in, but that he was quite well and unwounded. Many various, indifferent, and insignificant people appeared before him. He talked to them and discussed something trivial. They were preparing to go away somewhere. Prince Andrew dimly realized that all this was trivial and that he had more important cares, but he continued to speak, surprising them by empty witticisms. Gradually, unnoticed, all these persons began to disappear and a single question, that of the closed door, superseded all else. He rose and went to the door to bolt and lock it. Everything depended on whether he was, or was not, in time to lock it. He went, and tried to hurry, but his legs refused to move and he knew he would not be in time to lock the door though he painfully strained all his powers. He was seized by an agonizing fear. And that fear was the fear of death. *It* stood behind the door. But just when he was clumsily creeping toward the door, that dreadful something on the other side was already pressing against it and forcing its way in. Something not human—death—was breaking in through that door, and had to be kept out. He seized the door, making a final effort to hold it back—to lock it was no longer possible—but his efforts were weak and clumsy and the door, pushed from behind by that terror, opened and closed again.

Once again *it* pushed from outside. His last superhuman efforts were vain and both halves of the door noiselessly opened. *It* entered, and it was *death*, and Prince Andrew died.

But at the instant he died, Prince Andrew remembered that he was asleep, and at the very instant he died, having made an effort, he awoke.

"Yes, it was death! I died—and woke up. Yes, death is an awakening!" And all at once it grew light in his soul and the veil that had till then concealed the unknown was lifted from his spiritual vision. He felt as if powers till then confined within him had been liberated, and that strange lightness did not again leave him.

When, waking in a cold perspiration, he moved on the divan, Natásha went up and asked him what was the matter. He did not answer and looked at her strangely, not understanding.

That was what had happened to him two days before Princess Mary's arrival. From that day, as the doctor expressed it, the wasting fever assumed a malignant character, but what the doctor said did not interest Natásha, she saw the terrible moral symptoms which to her were more convincing.

From that day an awakening from life came to Prince Andrew together with his awakening from sleep. And compared to the duration of life it did not seem to him slower than an awakening from sleep compared to the duration of a dream.

There was nothing terrible or violent in this comparatively slow awakening.

His last days and hours passed in an ordinary and simple way. Both Princess Mary and Natásha, who did not leave him, felt this. They did not weep or shudder and during these last days they themselves felt that they were not attending on him (he was no longer there, he had left them) but on what reminded them most closely of him—his body. Both felt this so strongly that the outward and terrible side of death did not affect them and they did not feel it necessary to foment their grief. Neither in his presence nor out of it did they weep, nor did they ever talk to one another about him. They felt that they could not express in words what they understood.

They both saw that he was sinking slowly and quietly, deeper and deeper, away from them, and they both knew that this had to be so and that it was right.

He confessed, and received communion: everyone came to take leave of him. When they brought his son to him, he pressed his lips to the boy's and turned away, not because he felt it hard and sad (Princess Mary and Natásha understood that) but simply because he thought it was all that was required of him, but when they told him to bless the boy, he did what was demanded and looked round as if asking whether there was anything else he should do.

When the last convulsions of the body, which the spirit was leaving, occurred, Princess Mary and Natásha were present.

"Is it over?" said Princess Mary when his body had for a few minutes lain motionless, growing cold before them. Natásha went up, looked at the dead eyes, and hastened to close them. She closed them but did not kiss them, but clung to that which reminded her most nearly of him—his body.

"Where has he gone? Where is he now?..."

When the body, washed and dressed, lay in the coffin on a table, everyone came to take leave of him and they all wept.

Little Nicholas cried because his heart was rent by painful perplexity. The countess and Sónya cried from pity for Natásha and because he was no more. The old count cried because he felt that before long, he, too, must take the same terrible step.

Natásha and Princess Mary also wept now, but not because of their own personal grief; they wept with a reverent and softening emotion which had taken possession of their souls at the consciousness of the simple and solemn mystery of death that had been accomplished in their presence.